THE HENCHMAN TRAINING ACADEMY 2: EXPANSION

L.K. URBAN

The Henchman Training Academy 2: Expansion

EBook ISBN: 978-1-7364582-6-6
Trade Paperback ISBN: 978-1-7364582-7-3

Edited by Kailey Urbaniak
Cover design by Angela Stevens

Published by WIP Publications LLC
Colorado Springs, CO 80907
Kailey Urbaniak, Publisher

WIP Publications eBook Edition 2022
WIP Publications Trade Paperback Edition 2022
Printed in the USA

CONTENTS

CHAPTER 1
IT'S OUT OF MY HANDS

The Team meeting hadn't been the public lynching Matt was anticipating. Despite him having to stand in front of a room full of pissed off Henchmen, Matt silently congratulated himself for the heroics he performed. It was unexpected that Fowler asked him to address the Henchmen, but it worked out for the best. He didn't have time to worry and be anxious about choosing the right words to say. Instead, he worked off his intuition, which, as Jimmie would say, was the only way to go. The Henchmen seemed to have responded well to Matt calling out the lack of training before starting their jobs. Matt was relieved that it didn't come off as him being an educated snob, again. It helped that Franco had jumped in and publicly agreed with him. In a strange way, Matt hoped that what he offered had redeemed himself enough to stay in the House. He was finally getting used to the culture of the House, and the thought of going back to the boredom and dullness of his previous life frightened him more than anything.

The words Garrett, the DMF in-house council, spoke to him after the meeting were ringing in his head as the Global Conference Room emptied. Garrett had joked about a Henchman Training Academy, but Matt wasn't laughing. The idea intrigued him, and, if given the opportunity, it was something that could keep him in the House, maybe without having to carry a concealed weapon to work each day. Kill or be killed had worked this far to keep him in a balanced state of homeostasis but adding up his kill count wasn't a goal he strived for.

Liz waited near the door for Matt. He met up with her and she said, "I need a drink."

"You read my mind. Let's go!" Matt directed her toward the kitchen.

Liz grabbed some keys and the two of them headed to the nearby drive-through liquor store, Papa Jack's, to which they were frequent visitors, for good or bad. It made things easier to not have to get out of the car, which was always a good thing when Matt was around. Next stop was their favorite pizza from a place called Fat Sully's. Matt always ordered the pizza as soon as they left the House. By the time they made their way through Papa Jack's, the pizza was ready.

That night, they decided it would be best to take the pizza and beer up to his room since the conversation they wanted to have wasn't for everyone to hear. Some nights they would sit in the kitchen and hang with the other guys, but not tonight. They plopped down on Matt's bed. Matt opened two bottles of beer and handed one to Liz. As usual, they each reached out and tapped the necks of the beer bottles together, a silent 'cheers' to each other. They each took a big slug of beer, followed by a long, contented sigh.

"That is good," Matt said through a long, loud burp.

"Do you always have to burp with your mouth open? God, it's so nasty," Liz said as she opened the pizza box. "Now, that looks good."

"All good but the mushrooms." Matt grimaced.

"Nothing wrong with a few little veggies making their way into your body," Liz argued, grabbing herself a slice.

They both dug in, not realizing how hungry they were. Matt could put away serious amounts of food, and Liz didn't do too bad herself. They sometimes had to buy more than one pizza to fill them both up.

After the feeding frenzy, and a beer gone each, Liz asked, "So, did you just make the stuff up during the meeting?"

"What stuff? I meant the apology a hundred percent if that is what you mean," Matt said.

"Not that, I mean the stuff about gaps. Do you see gaps?"

"Oh, yeah, I do. I didn't mean for it to sound like it was bad, just observations I made. Did it come off like I'm trying to be smarter than everyone? I hope not, I'm tired of taking that rap."

"No, that wasn't it. I mean, it was good what you said. I think people know you well enough now to know where you are coming from. Overall, it was a good talk. I think that you bringing that up, the gaps, is what may have saved you from being asked to leave here," Liz said.

"Oh shit, I'm that close to being thrown out? I didn't realize I would be fired. I thought they would just put me in the kitchen or something, washing dishes. I guess I have no idea how people get fired from being Henchmen. Seems the only reason a Henchman would have to retire is when they are dead or severely disabled," Matt said.

Liz chuckled. "Yeah, being dead would lead to your career ending. I saw my dad and Jimmie leaving the GCR, they were talking, and I think that's a good sign."

Matt knew he was walking a fine line, but the thought of having to leave scared the shit out of him. He enjoyed his life at the House. Now that he was more accustomed to the lifestyle, he didn't want to leave. He wasn't used to failing and not being good at something.

"Liz, what advice do you have that may help convince your dad and uncle to give me just one more chance?" Matt asked.

Liz was always a difficult read, but when her foot began to tap, he knew she was speaking with more emotion that she knew what to do with. Before she answered, her foot started to bounce off the bottom edge of Matt's bed. "Sport, you may have to let the fates take over on this one. This is all unfamiliar territory. I'm even having trouble predicting the outcome on this one."

Matt had a mouthful of pizza, and he stopped chewing, replying without swallowing. "Would it be wise for me to ask to speak to them more directly? I know I can write up a fucking fantastic business plan. I have plenty of ideas, some of which would incorporate training Henchmen and ways to be more fiscally responsible. I did help my friends at The Basement grow their business with the business plan I developed."

"Why do you always do that, talking with your mouth full, yuck," Liz complained with her nose scrunched up. "But listen, it's a waiting game; the ball is in their court right now. It's my understanding that they would at least give you a chance to make any changes they suggest before firing you."

Matt sighed. "Bottom line, I hope they give me an opportunity to use my skills to help DMF."

Liz hopped off Matt's bed, rubbing her full belly. "I promise you that as soon as I hear anything, I will let you know." Liz paused, then said, "In a weird way, I feel hopeful, because what you spoke about doing was well overdue. I actually got excited thinking that we could literally revolutionize the role of Henchmen, which has been a very outdated profession."

As soon as Liz left, Matt's mind drifted off with visions of how he would change things up. He was going to wait until he heard whether he was free to create or doomed to be fed to the wolves.

After a restless night's sleep, Matt woke to quiet tapping on his door. It was so quiet, he wasn't sure if he was imagining it. His question was answered for him as Liz came in the door with two coffees and a big smile.

"Aren't you a happy camper today? A little earlier than I'm used to," Matt said in a sleepy tone.

Liz shushed him. "No one can know I'm here. Seriously, this must be on the down, down low. I even disabled the CCTV feed to your room and down the hall," she whispered.

Whispering back, Matt replied, "Got it, but what's the big deal? Are you planning my escape? Did things turn sour on me with your dad and uncle?"

Liz didn't answer as she made her way to the end of Matt's bed while he laid propped up with his many pillows.

"I slept like shit last night, it will be good to start the day on a more positive note," Matt said, taking the first sip of his coffee.

"Before I tell you, promise me you won't give any hint that we talked. I mean it. You have to put on a show when it comes to meeting with my dad and uncle," Liz demanded.

"Sure, I can do that," Matt promised. His heart was racing at the intensity of Liz's tone.

Liz made her way to lying next to Matt, getting comfortable with another set of pillows propped up behind her, noting that this would be a long story to tell. She said that both her dad and uncle had not taken this decision lightly. While in the office, her dad kept rubbing his temples, saying 'what the fuck' over and over, while her uncle paced the room in silence.

"They said that you broke rule number two, *never do an*

errand alone, but since that first time, you haven't done it again. Same with rules number one, *never speak on the job*, and number five, *know your role, stay in your lane.* They both agreed that you have rule number four down better than most, *never hesitate,* which is typically the most difficult one to train."

"That's all true, not going to argue that point," Matt conceded.

"But the good thing is they also noted that once you are told that you broke the rule, you never have to be reminded again. You get it after one time, which isn't always the case with most of the guys on the Team," Liz said. "They also see that you are loyal and come with good intentions about wanting to be a world-class Henchman. Where they are hesitant is they wonder whether working at DMF is your ultimate career goal, who you really strive to be."

"I'm not so sure it is," Matt said, sitting up and running his hands through his hair.

"I think this conversation would have happened anyway at some point."

"Yeah, me too, so what's next then, do I just wait to hear from them?" Matt asked.

"Yes, they will contact you to come meet with them. But you need to be cool, you understand?" Liz released her intense stare to look down as her phone buzzed with a text. "That's them, I need to go. This is going to be a good thing for you, Sport."

He let out a long sigh of relief. Things were lining up for him, no more Tailgaters Insurance, no more soul-sucking routine. Matt stood up and paced his room with anticipation and excitement about the day ahead. He knew he had to play it cool and pretend that nothing out of the ordinary had taken place this morning. With that in mind, he got ready to go downstairs for breakfast just like any other day. As he made his way down the stairs, he saw that the door to Fowler's office was closed, indicating that they were still discussing the next steps with Liz.

Matt entered the kitchen just in time to grab the last sesame bagel and another cup of coffee, saying good morning to Finch from the CM Team. Matt sat in his favorite chair that overlooked the garden in the back of the House. As if planned, when he took the last sip of coffee, his phone buzzed with a text from Jimmie requesting him to be in Fowler's office in five.

He cleared his plate and mug before walking slowly down the hallway.

Matt knocked lightly on the half-opened door of Fowler's office. "Come on in, Matt," Jimmie called.

Fowler, Jimmie, and Liz were sitting in the office looking relaxed as Matt walked in. Remembering the part he had promised Liz he would play, Matt came in wide-eyed, with hands in his pockets, and his eyes trained on nothing in particular. If Liz hadn't already told him this was going to be a positive conversation, he would never have been able to read any of their faces. They had all perfected the poker face.

"Have a seat," Fowler said, motioning to the last remaining open seat at his desk.

Matt sat, reminding himself to take a deep breath. He wasn't sure what they were going to say. Even though Liz seemed excited about it, Matt didn't know what this all meant for him and his future at DMF.

"Matt, do you truly love what you are doing here right now? In all honesty, can you picture yourself doing this job long-term, exactly as it is right now?" Jimmie asked. There were no niceties, chit chat, Jimmie got down to business.

The three waited intently for Matt's response. He weighed his answer carefully. Basically, he had nowhere else to go, he had gotten used to the lifestyle, the money, the lack of the nine-to-five gig. However, if he was to be honest, he did not love parts of it, and he was always noting ways he thought things should be, which made keeping his mouth shut as a Henchman every day even harder.

"That's a tough question, since I never saw myself doing a job like this, ever," Matt said. "I think I made the best of a difficult situation. I can tell you I never thought I would kill anyone, or that violence and the occasional killing would be a routine and expected part of my daily job. That has never felt right to me. Obviously, I have shown to have a knack for it, but for the rest of my life? No, this isn't my dream job. I'm more of a big picture guy. I don't see things moment by moment like the other Henchmen do. I admit that part does not come as natural to me."

Fowler narrowed his eyes and said, "Thank you for being transparent and for your thoughtful response. I'm relieved because I hoped that you didn't actually love what you did and thought you were good at it. This makes things a lot easier for both me and Jimmie."

Matt's forehead crinkled, and he turned to Jimmie for some clarification.

"We have created a role for you here, Matt. It's going to be up to you to agree with our terms. Hopefully, you will not find too much to disagree with."

With that, Matt allowed himself to make eye contact, first with Liz, then with Fowler. "A new role?"

"We know you are a hard worker with a respectful attitude. What we're proposing is what we see as a perfect marriage of your skills," Jimmie said. "We would like to have you, Matt, use your skill set and education to create some type of program that would help evaluate skills and to give training where there are gaps. One of the major initiatives is to reduce collateral damage and stress responses in some situations."

"That sounds exciting," Matt said, "but would I not be a full-time Henchman then? Does this mean you don't think I would ever be any good at that?"

"What it means," Jimmie replied, leaning forward, "is that we see your skill set, your education, and this is where we see you best fitting in. You are a unicorn here at DMF, no one has that background. We see that as your strongest asset."

"We would like you to be comfortable with this and get started working on a new role here right away," Fowler said. "If you accept this offer, you will need to be ready to present us your plan in two weeks' time."

"You know, I don't think that is going to work for me. I will have to decline your offer," Matt said with a serious look.

Fowler, Jimmie, and Liz's eyes darted to each other, then back to Matt. All three were confused by his unexpected answer. Liz was the first to speak, "Are you fucking nuts? What do you think you're doing? This is a great offer; I don't understand."

Matt let his smile crack. "Sorry, that was a failed attempt at humor, it was funny to see your reactions though. It is rare to see any sort of expressions on your faces. But yes of course, I accept. I can definitely do that. I appreciate this opportunity to continue on with DMF," Matt replied enthusiastically. Matt felt like he had just gotten a promotion in a career field that didn't really offer promotions. Immediately, the first thought that popped into his head was Garrett's joking idea of a Henchman Training Academy.

No one else looked amused by Matt's joke.

"Keep in mind, you're not off the hook yet. This is another hoop you have to jump through to earn your place in DMF," Fowler added.

"I like the idea, I won't lie, but I also have a request to make," Matt said, looking over to see Liz shaking her head side to side, as if to say, *no, no more jokes, this isn't the time or place for that.*

"Go on," Jimmie said, "Tell us what you have in mind."

"Since this is a big job, I'm going to need some help. I haven't been a Henchman all that long, really. I request that Liz be freed up to work with me at least until we get the new system in place, to help with the creative side of it," Matt proposed.

Liz looked up with surprise and tried to conceal her smile. Matt knew she was interested in being more than her dad's Henchman, and that this would be a perfect opportunity to have her shift into a modern new role.

"Liz? There would be some consequences of her moving to your new Team. I'm not opposed to the idea, but we will need to discuss further," Fowler replied, looking to his daughter.

"I understand I just threw you a curve ball. I'm good with waiting on your decision, I know it will have a ripple effect on the Team," Matt said.

"We will get back with you on this. If you could excuse us now?" Jimmie asked.

Matt strutted back to his room feeling proud that he had not only played the innocent, but that he had dropped a bomb not even Liz saw coming.

He sat at his desk to play a quick game of COD to get his mind off the stress of the day. He had his headphones on and was completely gone to the outside world, in his safety zone, or just plain old mental escaping.

As the day turned into night, and the night turned into day, Matt emerged from his self-induced gaming coma. *Did I really give up a night's sleep for this*? Matt yawned and stretched his long legs.

Coffee, yes, coffee was just what he needed. On his way down to the kitchen, Franco and David H. were just finishing up their breakfast.

"You look like shit, College Boy. Did you have scary dreams last night, miss your mommy?" David H. sneered.

"Shave much, dude? You look rough man," Franco added.

"Good morning to you too. Nothing going on that a little coffee won't fix," Matt said.

"No Pinky's today? Is that what is scaring you, College Boy?" David H. asked.

"Oh shit, I didn't even think of that. I was in the zone for the last twelve hours," Matt replied.

"What do you mean, in the zone? Is that a gaming term for pissing away twelve hours of your life?" Franco asked.

"It means he forgot about the real world and disappeared into his gaming world. Are you sure you aren't on the CM Team? What a fucking nerd you are," David H. laughed.

"You think since you're a gamer you don't need to work out anymore?" Franco taunted.

Matt smiled. "I'm not trying to skip out on anything. Plus, you guys would miss me coming to Pinky's with you. Let me go grab my gear, meet you in the back."

"You have two minutes, then we're out," Franco said.

"And you don't want to leave your little gym girlfriend hanging, do you, Lover Boy?" David H. snickered.

"Boys! How lovely to see you three handsome men today! How are things at the House, Eddie doing ok?" Pinky called to them.

Matt always liked the feel of walking into Pinky's. It was not one of those huge impersonal gyms that was too crowded with people more interested in finding a date than they were in working out. Since it was in a strip mall, the front was all windows, which made it bright with natural light, not like the big chain gyms that were filled with loads of florescent bulbs. There were few regular people who came to Pinky's who weren't from the Team. Amber was one of the few who was considered a regular. Matt had had a crush on Amber since the moment he'd laid eyes on her a few months ago. She was there now, taking a sip from her water bottle near the squat racks.

"Hey Pinky, yes things are going well both with Fowler, and at the House. What's new here?" Franco asked.

"Same old, same old. Nothing exciting here. In case you didn't already notice, she's here too." Pinky nodded toward Amber, who was removing a plate from the squat rack. Of course, Matt had already seen her the moment he walked in. His attention was laser focused on watching her every move, totally distracted from being part of the conversation.

"Yeah, I saw her. College Boy over here is already drooling. You're ridiculous, man," David H. said, punching Matt in the arm.

"Huh? What, I'm sorry, I didn't hear anything you said," Matt said, still wide eyed.

"You are dismissed, College Boy; you can go to her. Have a nice workout with little Miss Redhead," Franco teased.

Matt jumped at the chance to spend some uninterrupted time with Amber. Lately, she had been working out there at the same time, always leaving right as they came in.

Before Matt could make his move, Amber walked up to the men. Amber smiled, looking directly at Matt. "Hey fellas, Matt, good to see you, it's been a while. Too bad I can't stay. I was just on my way out. We could have done a workout together. Maybe next time."

"Next time," Matt mumbled. "Have a good day, Amber."

David H. started laughing before Amber had taken another step. "Burned College Boy, guess you are back with us."

"That was a quick burn, wasn't it? Let's get to it," Matt sighed.

The workout gave Matt just enough energy to make it through the rest of the day. Just before dinner, the adrenaline was gone, and with the lack of sleep from the night before, Matt crashed.

CHAPTER 2
OFF AND RUNNING

Early the next morning, Matt was startled awake by the sight of Liz sitting on the edge of his bed with an emotionless expression. It was unnerving to think Liz could always sneak into his room while he was sleeping, and he was completely oblivious. Liz said nothing as he sat up, rubbing his eyes. She must know what Fowler and Jimmie decided, but was she pissed at him? He looked up, searching her eyes for any bit of a tell. *Shit, she's too good at keeping her face unreadable.* He got nothing from her.

Matt quickly removed his headphones. "What, no coffee today? I could use some."

"They want to talk to you," Liz said, stone faced. That was it. No other clues. Matt was desperate to see any spec of information on Liz's face, but it was devoid of any signs, a look he knew her to have perfected.

Liz left the room first. Matt immediately rolled out of bed, stopped to pee and splash water on his face and hair, threw on a t-shirt and jeans, and obediently followed Liz down the stairs to Fowler's office. He wondered why she didn't wait for him, give him a quick pep talk, or anything. This had to be bad news.

Matt's nerves were getting the best of him. He was shaking

enough to make him have to grab the handrail on the way down the stairs. He was repeating, *control what you can control,* to himself over and over until he reached the door.

As he entered the office, Jimmie was standing with the scary, patented DMF death stare. Arms crossed across his chest, Fowler was seated at his desk, looking agitated. Matt could not read what was going on, and when he turned to look at Liz, he saw her quietly exiting the room and shutting the door behind her.

Oh, fuck. I bet she can't be here when they kick my ass out. If it was good news, wouldn't she have stayed, and wouldn't they both look a little more relaxed? He stared at his feet.

"Hey kid, best to keep your head up until we're done talking. We're negotiating here. Gotta learn to play the game," Fowler said.

Matt forced himself to look up. "You're right, I need to work on my facial expressions if I'm to stay in this line of work," Matt agreed. He had been fairly certain that the worst possible outcome of this negotiation would be that he would be expected to create this new training academy alone. From the way things were left, this was just a matter of asking Liz to exchange her current role to the development end of DMF. But feeling the vibes that these two men were throwing off made him feel unsettled.

Fowler sighed and gave Jimmie a quick glance. The silence was heavy. Matt couldn't sit still. "Jimmie and I have made a decision about your proposal," Fowler said finally. "We just don't think it's going to work out."

"Which part will not work out?" asked a panicked Matt.

"The part about you continuing trying to fit in as a Henchman. It's time to give it up. It just isn't for you, and after hearing how you felt about the role, it just makes little sense to keep you on that track," Fowler responded.

Matt couldn't keep his head from dropping back down. "Then what makes sense?" he asked quietly.

"We want you to create a training program," Jimmie said. Matt's head shot up, feeling relieved. "We also want you to work with Liz for a couple of reasons. The first being you need her in-depth experience as a Henchman to help know what you don't know, and the second is that we see this as a way for her to expand her skill set as well."

Taking a long breath, Matt smiled and said, "The first class should be 'How to have an emotionless face and other negotiating skills.'" Both Jimmie and Fowler cracked a smile. "Thank you for the opportunity, I accept your offer. I look forward to making this a huge global success. I won't disappoint."

Matt rose to give them each a handshake before departing.

Exiting the meeting, Matt hoped that Liz was standing right outside the door or on the couch. He wanted to give her some shit for not letting him know what was about to be dropped in his lap. He took a quick glance around, no Liz.

He started to head back to his room, and as he turned the corner to enter his room, there was Liz, standing with a bright smile. She covered her mouth with her hands, as if to hide her excitement. Liz jumped up and hugged Matt, knocking him off balance. He didn't see that reaction coming. It was a quick embrace that made Matt smile. "I would love to help you develop your plan, Matt! The thought of helping you and my family's company to step up into the twenty-first century is an opportunity I can't pass on."

"Down girl!" Matt laughed. He was still peeved that she had such a good poker face. "Hey, can we make a deal?" Matt asked.

Liz smirked. "Depends on the deal, Sport. What kinda deal are we talking about?"

"Friends don't let friends be victims of the curse of the

DMF poker face. Can you please promise to never pull that on me ever again?" Matt asked.

Liz rolled her eyes and said, "The curse is a family tradition, I'm not sure that I can promise to never, ever do it again. But what I can promise is that I'll only pull it out in case of an emergency."

"I'll take that, it's a start," Matt said.

Matt's mind was already chasing some ideas as they walked to his room together. He was grateful he would have Liz to bounce some of them off, as he trusted and valued her opinion.

"Let's meet up in the morning to get to work," Liz said. Matt nodded in agreement. "You know, Sport, just because they're letting us work on this task doesn't mean they're going to implement it if we don't make a compelling plan. Plus, you haven't proven yourself yet in their minds. There's a lot riding on this for you. But I'm glad you're not being thrown to the wolves just yet."

"Believe me, I know. We're going to have to show them a kick-ass business plan."

"I've never done something like this. I've always wanted to, but never had a reason to. I'm excited, but I'll let you take the lead on this, Sport. Just let me know how I can help, and I will," Liz said. With that, Liz turned to leave but stopped after a few steps to face Matt again. "We're going to rock their world with this, it's going to be so fucking cool."

Exhausted but happy, Matt literally fell into his bed. He laid for a second and thought how fucking strange his life had become. With this opportunity, he had a chance settle into his comfort zone for at least the next two weeks. This project would be a pleasant distraction from his stress about making more mistakes.

———

Matt woke from a restless sleep and wanted to start his day off with a quick lift. He knew he would be in a better place, more mentally focused, if he put some time in at the gym. Pinky's had become more than a workout for him ever since he saw Amber. They hadn't made it past small talk, but Matt could not take his eyes off her. He had been the victim of endless razzing by the Team about his inability to make the first move by asking her out on a date. Everyone could see there was an attraction on both ends. Matt blamed his inability to ask Amber on a date on Jimmie's instruction to proceed with caution until he could find out more about her, but really, Matt wasn't sure if he'd be able to work up the courage to ask her out anyway.

Realistically, Matt knew it didn't take this long to run a background check on anyone. Shit, it had taken them minutes to know his identity the night he brought Fowler back from the Basement. There must be either a crazy complex, twisted story about Amber's past that they didn't want to share, or they found nothing, and they didn't want to let him know he was right about her; she was not a threat in anyway.

This time, Matt saw Amber as he, Franco, and David H. were leaving, *I can't wait to laugh at all of them when they finally come clean and tell me they found nothing on her.*

"Hey Matt," Amber said with a sweet, coy smile.

"Amber, how's it going?" Matt stammered, pausing awkwardly in the middle of the doorway. As he turned back to look at Amber, he forgot to put a hand on the door, and the glass door smacked into the side of his face.

"It's going," she laughed. She turned as Pinky started waving hello to her. "Have a good day!"

"You too," Matt mumbled, rubbing his cheek. Both Franco and David H. were rolling their eyes, David H. pretending to vomit.

"Come on, get out of the doorway, Lover Boy," Franco said.

Before he lost his nerve, Matt called to Amber, "Our timing is off, we keep missing each other. Maybe we can plan to be here at the same time? Can I text you or something?"

Both Franco and David H. raised their eyebrows.

Amber's smile grew wider. "Let's try that, you know how to find my number, looks like your boys want to leave."

"I do?" Matt asked.

"If you ask Pinky, I'm sure she can help you out with that," she called with a wink. "Bye for now!"

Matt received double arm punches from Franco and David H. on the walk to the car.

First thing after Pinky's and a shower, Liz and Matt had scheduled a meeting to begin their strategy planning. Not wanting to be late, Matt skipped out on his usual morning coffee to head straight there.

Liz had gotten to the meeting room first, the same room Matt had had his meeting with Franco and David H. weeks ago, pleading with them to be more inclusive. She'd brought in some snacks and had put a pot of coffee on before Matt got there. Liz had gigantic Post-it notes set up on an easel lots of markers scattered around.

"Thank you for getting this all set up, I couldn't have done better myself. This is all we really need," Matt said, opening his laptop.

"I'm glad you think so. I've been thinking nonstop about how to get this thing off the ground," Liz said.

"We have all the tools we need, which is awesome. I've been thinking too, and I was wondering what your thoughts are on me speaking with Franco about this, just to get some feedback and information about things he sees as gaps."

"Franco, yes, maybe him, but please no David H. I think the fewer people with eyes on this, the better, for now at least. Franco is a natural leader and gets it, you know?"

"I agree. I'll set something up with just Franco next time I can get him alone."

Just as he had done with his college presentations and quarterly progress reports at Tailgaters, Matt began by noting some fundamental ideas and capturing them onto the large Post-it notes. Matt chuckled to himself, thinking of the research papers and other projects he had to create in college. What a trip this was. He couldn't imagine handing in something like this to his professor. Just the title would make them question their own sanity, *The Henchman Training Academy*?

They worked most of the day with brief breaks to walk around, stretch their legs, and get fresh air. Their focus for this first day was to identify what the current state of DMF was. As they summarized the issues, it all boiled down to it really being a free for all, with no structure or protocol. Natural leaders rose to the top, but with no training, everyone was just working off instinct. Another big problem was there had to be some management of the trauma associated with the constant stress that the job brought.

As the sun set, Matt and Liz called it quits for the day. They stood and looked at the many large Post-its that had started out blank, but now were full of newly generated ideas. Both were satisfied with the amount of work done on day one. Matt stood next to Liz, staring proudly at the sight of all their work. Matt put his hand in the air, showing that he wanted to exchange high fives with Liz.

"You are such a dork," Liz laughed, slapping his hand.

"Aw, come on dude, just excited," Matt said, smiling. "I'm cooked, I just want to shut my eyes and get ready for tomorrow."

"Let me make sure the digital lock still works on this door. We haven't used it for so long, I'm not sure I remember the code," Liz said pushing the lock button. "What's the code again? Oh yeah, I know, let me try this."

The lock opened with the numbers Liz pressed. "Nice," Matt said. "Our secret is safe."

Matt and Liz looked over to the kitchen to see if there was any food left for dinner. Franco was sitting in the kitchen alone, finishing up what looked like a large bowl of ice cream. Matt knew that this would be a perfect time to talk to Franco and get him up to speed on his latest project and to explain why Matt's name wouldn't be on the Errand Board any longer.

Liz nudged him, nodded toward Franco.

"Christ, I'm tired, but what the fuck? I'm on it, I'll talk to you in the morning," Matt said to Liz, walking over to Franco's table. "Hey man, that looks good, is there any food left?" Matt asked Franco.

"Yeah, I think there is. It's a little late for dinner though. I see you and Miss Perfect are having another secret meeting behind closed doors. Must be something special," Franco said.

"Actually, it is, and it's something I wanted to speak to you about. Do you have a couple minutes to spare? I think you'll find this is worth your while," Matt said. Franco nodded, and Matt sat across from him. "Franco, I have some pretty fantastic news to share with you about what Liz and I have been working on. It involves the Team and a sort of new, unique structure. We wanted to get your input on our ideas because you are the highest-ranking Team member."

"Highest-ranking, really? I'm not sure about that," laughed Franco. "But sure, I would love to hear what you're putting together. I figured something was up after the last Team meeting."

"Liz and I have been creating something that will have

long-term implications on our field of work. We're excited about the progress. We haven't shared this information with anyone, and we haven't even presented it to Fowler or Jimmie yet," Matt said.

"Cool, we can chat for a bit. I do have to get home tonight though, or Syd will have my head," Franco replied, glancing at the time on his watch.

"I'll keep it short," Matt promised. "You know, I hardly know anything about you and how you ended up here. I know you're married, and I've heard you talking to David H. about your daughter. How do you explain this job to your family?"

"Yes, I have a family. As far as how I started out here, you might be surprised to know our stories didn't start out so different. I was a jock too, a basketball player. I was even a college boy like yourself, for a time," Franco said.

"No shit, really? I had no idea. Did you get your degree?" Matt asked.

"No, I left after a few semesters with a wife and daughter, Sydney and Emmie. I got a degree in being a family man. No regrets," Franco said.

"No regrets, that's good. Does your wife, Sydney, know what you do for work?"

"To be honest, at first she didn't. We were so broke after we had Emmie. When I was asked to come join DMF, I was afraid to tell her. I thought she would freak, and I would have to go back to working two shit jobs, making not even half of what I bring home now. It took me some time to explain it to her in a way that she would understand."

"I bet that was an intense conversation. That was a lot to keep from her," Matt said.

"It was. But I dreamt of having Sydney stay home with Emmie and having a comfortable life. I quickly learned that I couldn't come home and have a 'gee honey, how was your day' conversation. I tried to make my stories a PG version of what really went down. I kept my daily activities vague and not specific. It seemed to work, but I felt guilty about not telling her the truth. Sydney was so happy staying at home. I finally had to come clean and tell her everything, well mostly everything, about what I did every day."

"For what it's worth, I think you did the right thing. But what do you tell your friends about your job?" Matt asked.

"Sydney and I came up with a story together. Basically, I work security for an international business. We don't say more than that. I am pretty sure that is what a lot of the other guys on the Team say as well," Franco said.

"That works for me, and in reality, it isn't too far from the truth," Matt said.

"So, you see, I'm not that different from you. Instead of a college degree, I learned how to provide for my family financially. Sydney doesn't always agree with what I do, but we have gotten used to the lifestyle the money affords us." Franco reached into his pocket and pulled out his phone, showing Matt a picture of a pretty young woman holding a laughing toddler who strongly resembled Franco.

"You can definitely tell that's your daughter, that's so cool. I always thought I would be a dad someday," Matt said, smiling.

"It's great being a dad, it just scares me sometimes to think of leaving her and Sydney. One of the worst conversations I have ever had was when I had to call her and tell her I'd gotten hurt on the job. It's different when you have a family.

"Christ, I feel like such an asshole," Matt said, hanging his head in shame. "I still feel a huge amount of responsibility for you getting injured. I still don't know what I was thinking." Matt shuddered as he recalled Franco being shot by the OT, while he and David H. watched. It was all because of Matt's bad judgement, going off script. The OT had missed his shot aimed at Matt and it'd hit Franco in the shoulder.

"I've already told you it wasn't your fault," Franco said, rolling his eyes. "Anyway, enough of that shit, what is the project they have you working on?"

Matt went into as much detail about the plans as he could. He went so far as to call it a Henchman Training Academy. He explained the concepts behind training and education for Henchmen, along with the intention to legitimize the profession.

"Are you shitting me? They bought that crap we talked about? I'm impressed, dude," Franco said, finishing the last of his mint chocolate chip ice cream.

"They bought it and have given me the freedom to create it from scratch. What I'm looking for is some insight and feedback from you, a veteran member of the DMF Henchman Team," Matt said.

"Insight and feedback about what exactly?"

"We want to know what your thoughts are about adding some structure and framework to it. Things like how to assess for readiness, what would we look for?" Matt asked.

"Off the top of my head, I would say we would want to get an idea about the skill level and strengths and weaknesses of each Henchman. That will help us determine where they should be assigned. We want all our Henchmen to work in the specialty they feel most drawn to," Franco said.

Matt nodded. "That's perfect, just what Jimmie was trying to figure out."

"To me it really does make sense. Some guys really hate doing certain jobs that others love. Why not have the guys doing more of what they like to do? I'll definitely help get some intel for you," Franco said.

"I think that would really be helpful and what we need to

get this thing started off right. Overall, you know the guys better than anyone else," Matt said.

Franco cracked a smile. "This is going to flip their lives upside down in a good way, I think. I don't think anyone has ever asked them what they like. Throw in a little training, and we can dominate!"

CHAPTER 3
THE BIG REVEAL

The pace was frenzied, but two weeks to the day, the presentation was complete, the meeting was set, and the nerves were raw.

"Are you sure Franco is going to be ready for this?" Liz asked.

"He's fine, don't worry about him. He's excited to share the suggestions he got from the Team. I like the abbreviation they came up with, the HTA, instead of having to say the Henchman Training Academy every time," Matt said.

Liz nodded. "I agree, the HTA has a nice ring to it. I also liked his suggestion to rank them according to their skill level. I'm thinking Jimmie will like the structure that brings."

As Matt and Liz made their way to the meeting room, they heard before they saw David H. and Franco in a heated discussion.

"What the fuck, dude? Where are you going now? Why are you dressed in a suit? We don't have anything on the board today. I've about had it with all this fucking secrecy," shouted a frustrated David H.

"Cool your shit down, David. I told you a million times,

once this meeting is done today, I'll be able to tell you everything," Franco said.

"I don't like my partner working behind my back, so what-the-fuck-ever, have fun with your new friends. Maybe Matt can be your new number two," David H. said before storming off.

"Everything ok here?" Liz asked.

"It *will* be. He's just a little freaked out and doesn't understand. I don't blame him. I'll be glad when I can make things right with him," Franco said.

"I can see why he's pissed off, he probably thinks the worst. After this, you go make nice," Liz said.

"I'm sorry dude, this has put you in the middle, making him feel left out. I didn't mean for that to happen," Matt said.

"Yeah, it's been rough. I'm not a good secret keeper when it comes to friends," Franco said.

Matt clapped Franco on the back. "You'll get to fix things with him soon. But for now, let's do this," Matt threw the doors open to the meeting room.

As they laid the information packets on the large conference room table, Fowler and Jimmie entered and sat down in the large, oversized leather chairs.

"We're looking forward to hearing what you have to say," Jimmie said while unconsciously paging through the packet in front of him.

"We're excited to begin. We've worked hard the last few days. Franco has been a great addition to our new HTA development Team," Matt said.

"HTA? I suppose you will get to the meaning?" Fowler asked.

"Absolutely we will, shall we get started?" Liz said. Fowler and Jimmie sat watching Liz begin the presentation with a sense of pride, their faces gentle and soft. It was one of the first times

Matt could read what they were thinking. She continued, "Our focus was identifying gaps that occur while on the job. Garrett let us review the recorded incidents for the last several months. We will be calling them 'case studies' from here on. While reviewing several case studies, we found it was the Henchmen's hyperreactivity that has led to the most costly mistakes."

"Costly?" Fowler said.

Liz said, "Most of the costs went to things like replacing damaged property, replacing cars after reckless driving, medical bills, and payouts to the families, which has led to unnecessary financial drain for DMF."

"I'm sure that's a fuck-ton of money tossed out to cover those expenses," Fowler growled.

"It is," Matt began, "but the good news is that we have developed a plan to get out from underneath the heavy financial burden. The HTA, The Henchman Training Academy. This would be an opportunity to train the Henchmen to become experts in their specialized field and learn a fresh way to be Henchmen, to break the tradition, to tidy up what they do. Right now, there is no accountability, no reason for them to want to be better and improve their skills."

"A training academy? For Henchmen? That is fucking awesome. I can see where you are going with this. Better training, better at their jobs, less fucking messes to clean up," Fowler said.

Franco cleared his throat as if to ask permission to speak. Matt nodded, smiling. "After speaking with the Team, the lack of a training protocol is a big issue. For the most part, they want to learn how to be better, but have nowhere to go to find out how. The better we become, the safer we are, which will trickle down to our families feeling more secure that we will come home at night," Franco said.

"Within the HTA, there will be a level of leadership that

will require specific qualities. Leaders will be identified and trained on how to lead and stick to the protocol. Adding structure is important," Liz added.

"Along with the structure, adding benefits would also lessen the financial impact. Anyone who enrolls and completes the HTA will be eligible for health insurance, PTO—paid time off—and life insurance. This way, all DMF would be responsible for would be monthly premiums, nothing out of pocket and unplanned for," Matt said.

"This all sounds well thought out and detailed. I like what I'm hearing. I have a strong sense that this will shine a light on Henchmen so they will be seen as more reputable. Can you explain more of the details of the HTA itself so we can get a better feel for what that would look like?" Jimmie said.

"Sure, let me start," Matt said. He explained that first, they would improve the onboarding process, meaning, they would actually have one. All new hires to DMF would be required to attend the HTA. The HTA will have some core required classes, like History of Henchmen, Addressing the Comic Book Side of the Field, The Five Rules of Being a Henchman, Company Benefits, How to Describe Your Job to Your Community, How to Manage Your Stress. In these classes, the goal would be to help all Henchmen find their 'whys,' what motivates them, all while doing some team building focused on making being a Henchman a legitimate career. The training videos would be out-of-class work to watch and come to class prepared to talk about. All the attendees would also have some basic physical education classes such as hand to hand combat, weapon handling, and the importance of working out and eating well.

"You two have been thorough. I have to say, teaching these big boys how to have a healthy diet may be the most difficult task you have proposed so far," laughed Fowler.

"That could be a challenge, that's for sure," Jimmie agreed.

"Franco will be conducting interviews with each student and determining which track or specialty they will move to after completing the core classes. We want the Henchmen to work in positions they feel connected to. To name a few examples of tracks to follow, we would have: advanced combatives, explosives, coding and IT systems, cyber security, foreign languages, negotiating deals, and defensive driving using a GPS," Matt said.

"We're also going to set up a quarterly physical test for everyone. This will, hopefully, keep them motivated. The CM Team will be required to do their own level of physical fitness too," Liz said.

"Having people work at the top of their game means only greater overall success and functionality. I think we can all agree on that," Jimmie said.

"With the creation of the HTA there would be a shift away from the explosive reactivity of the Henchman, leading to a reduced financial strain on DMF as well as a reduction in collateral damage. I think we all agree that those are important long-term goals," Matt said.

Franco continued, "The HTA will address the variety of needs of the modern-day Henchman. I think I speak for the rest of the Team when I say we want to make this profession more reputable, not the bad press that ends up in the movies, where the Henchmen always mess up and are just big reckless idiots. Most people only think they exist in comic books and Hollywood. Back when Henchmen were first used, the world was a different place. Now, a person can look around and find a Henchman in just about any company, business, and even in politics. Let's put some teeth into the profession and give it more credibility by providing a place for Henchmen to learn their trade."

Fowler and Jimmie nodded appreciatively.

"This could turn into a whole new business for DMF to start training Henchmen from other organizations, solo Henchmen, or whomever shows up. DMF would be able to earn back the investment by cutting down on costly errors and with the money made from the academy," Liz said.

"Like I said at the last Team meeting, becoming an expert in what you do is something we all should strive for. The HTA is positioned to offer the attendees the tools to get there." Matt smiled in Liz's direction, letting her know to go it was time to wrap up the presentation like they'd practiced.

Liz smiled back. "As we conclude our presentation, I want to state the obvious here. We all know that I have had more years of experience in the field than my partner, and even Franco. I want to ask that you fully endorse this project. I know my way around this field better than most, and I think it would benefit DMF tremendously. It has been an incredible experience for me to imagine and dream big. I will leave you with this thought: I truly believe that the HTA is a global endeavor. One day, this will be opened up to other Henchmen, making this available to Henchmen worldwide."

Fowler raised his eyebrows and Jimmie smiled widely.

Matt added, "'Let's be the best we can be,' is the motto, or tag line, that we would like to use as reinforcement and a bonding theme. It may sound cheesy, but we would like to use this motto on all of our swag." His words left a minute of silence in the room as everyone digested the presentation.

"We have a lot to process and digest," Jimmie said. "I have to be honest, I had not envisioned such a well-crafted presentation. The overall scope of this has exceeded any expectations I had about this project."

"Generally, we approve of the idea," Fowler said, looking to Jimmie who confirmed with a nod. "But as I'm sure you expected, we will need time to meet alone to discuss further and to think of questions to pose. You just laid some heavy shit on us."

"Thank you for your time and the opportunity to work on this. We're excited to hear what you think about it," Matt said.

Matt, Liz, and Franco excused themselves and headed toward the kitchen. Matt didn't have a good read on Fowler and Jimmie's thoughts. None of them had an appetite. Stress had made itself known physically, wreaking havoc with their digestion.

"How do you think that went over?" Matt asked, looking intently into Liz's eyes, searching for any hints.

"I think we shocked the hell out of them. I don't think they knew what we were going to propose, but they're definitely intrigued," Liz replied.

Matt turned to Franco. "Hey man, thank you for coming in with us. It was great to have your support. How do you think it went?"

"Having never been involved with anything like this, as far as I can tell, it was well received. And hey, I should be the one thanking you guys for the experience," Franco said, clapping Matt and Liz on the back.

Fowler and Jimmie purposely made them wait for what felt like an excruciating length of time. It wasn't until after lunch that Fowler called Matt and Liz back in. Franco had been excused the rest of the afternoon to continue his usual errands.

Back in Fowler's office, Jimmie jumped right in. "Right now, our top concern about all this change is how the rest of the Team will receive this. I could see some of them taking offense to this, saying they aren't good at their jobs, especially coming from you, Matt. Do you have any ideas on how you will get the others to 'buy in?'"

"That is an excellent question, and one we put thought into as well," Matt responded. "Our initial plan would be to get a few of the veteran guys in to meet. During this meeting, we would go over how they ended up being good at whatever it was they were good at and use them as examples and role models. If it was peer led, it would help with 'buy-in."

Jimmie nodded. "If this is presented to them in a way that reflects them being chosen by an intense selection process as leaders at DMF, then I think we will have a winning idea."

"I agree. We need to let them know what an honor it is to be selected to represent the first class of graduates of the HTA," Fowler said.

"I speak from experience when I say these guys will eat up the positive attention, which in turn will get everyone else to be curious about the HTA," Liz said.

"There is a fine line between making them feel like they have been inadequate and encouraging them to learn more and to identify the leadership qualities they possess," Jimmie added.

"I can't help going back to the financial aspect," Fowler said. He held up the numbers of the existing business plan. "These numbers make me a little sick to my stomach when I see the absolute amount of waste within our current model. What I liked the most was the benefits package. It's hard to argue with the numbers when you spell out just how much money we spend as opposed to what it would cost to offer benefits. Plus, the addition of benefits would go a long way to making it a legitimate profession and less comic bookish. However, this plan costs a lot of money to execute. We're not going to see a huge return on investment for a few years."

Jimmie nodded. "We need to hear more about the specific financial costs of getting this built and created."

"Absolutely," Matt said. "We are still talking to the contractors about how much the buildings would cost to remodel. We will let you know of the estimate."

Liz spoke up, "And, if we were to take this global, we would be able to earn back the investment much quicker." Jimmie and Fowler raised their eyebrows, looking to one another. "Yes, I said global. We aren't the only place that has Henchmen that need training. We could tap into the European market, and even the Henchmen for Hire message boards on the dark web."

Fowler pursed his lips and tapped his pen against the table. "I'm hesitant to look at this model as global. How are guys like that supposed to sit in the same room, then be expected to go hurt and possibly kill each other? I prefer it as an in-house program in the beginning, at least until we could get the kinks out."

Matt opened his mouth to answer, but Liz held her hand up to stop him. "I got this question, Matt. I see going global as a trickle-down effect with the training making a difference in the quality of work across the globe. Only an unaffiliated Henchman could come to the Academy. There wouldn't be tension as they don't have any loyalties yet. Everyone would learn the same skills, but with less violence. Overall, it would save money for all, and enable all the Henchmen to handle situations less like comic book characters and more like real professionals."

"Interesting angle, Liz," Fowler said, writing into his notebook.

Jimmie sat up and listened intently. "Talking about trauma or emotions has always been taboo and considered off limits with the Team, but if everyone was among peers with a shared experience, I find this could be a powerful concept. I would like to include stress reducers, like learning to breathe correctly and to meditate. I think our current practice of moving through the emotions with little connection to the event was an easy fix. I could never get a clear picture how to process this on such a large scale with all the Team. It just made sense to teach them how to shove things down, and to minimize. Obviously not mentally healthy, but the best solution I could come up with."

"Jimmie, it was the best thing at the time. If you would have had better tools, you would have offered them to us," Liz said.

"Which is why we have included you in the holistic portion of the HTA, Jimmie. You are the expert. We would be grateful for your participation," Matt added. Matt hadn't thought about going that far into the woo-woo shit that Jimmie swore by. He hadn't exactly embraced Jimmie's Eastern philosophies with much gusto. However, Matt knew those types of practices would fall in line with the overall goal, the idea of breathwork and meditation could be offered to graduates of the academy. Since Jimmie was unquestionably the expert, it made sense for him to oversee getting the mind–body connection part of the Academy up and running.

"I would be honored to at least be used as a consultant," Jimmie answered.

"Having Jimmie on board sounds like a dream job for him," Fowler said with a slight grin, "but what I want to know is what the timeline would be to get the Academy up and running. How soon do you think that could happen?"

Matt and Liz had prepped for this question and could say with confidence that given three to four months, it would be fully up and operational. As with any contracting job, they figured the only thing they wouldn't have control over was the speed of the construction on the remodel. Other than that, they had a good idea of how they wanted to structure the courses offered.

"This all sounds good, but none of it matters if we can't get the Team on board. We would first need more information on how this would be presented and then integrated into DMF. Having the Team be one hundred percent behind this concept is key to others at DMF following suit. These are the keys to the HTA's success. The other things will work themselves out," Jimmie said.

All nodded in agreement. "Now, you two get outta here. You both did a wonderful, comprehensive job on this. I can hardly imagine what we will sit here talking about a year from now," Fowler said.

Matt and Liz looked at each other, nodded in agreement, and got up to leave. Matt didn't know fully what the future held for either of them, but he felt proud of their presentations.

Outside, Matt turned to Liz. "We killed it!" he said enthusiastically. "Did you see their faces? They were *so* thinking about it. I really think they saw the potential for the Academy to revolutionize the way they conduct business."

"I think you're right. I know them pretty fucking well, and the looks we got were not you two are fucking nuts' looks. They are seriously considering it," Liz said, sighing loudly. "Are you hungry? Make the call."

Matt called Fat Sully's and placed an order for two large pepperoni, sausage, and mushroom pizzas. Matt splurged and got extra cheese on one, Liz laughed at him being so bold as she pulled into Papa Jack's, ordering two six-packs of Blue Moon.

CHAPTER 4
WE'VE GOT SOME WORK TO DO

Matt, Liz, and Franco met the next morning over breakfast and coffee to discuss strategy on how to win the Team over when presenting the HTA.

"We are definitely the best people to present this idea to the Team because we've had to work to win over the group. And Franco, you just have that 'it' factor with the Team," Liz said with air quotes.

Matt agreed. After all, they were both familiar with the dynamics of being an outsider, yearning to be accepted by the group.

"You know, when I first started, I too had to prove myself over and over with the guys. First, because I'm a girl, and second, because I'm related to the top two leaders of DMF," Liz confided.

"When I came on, I had questions about how you would do with the Team. But it didn't take long to see you could handle your business," Franco said, looking intently at Liz.

"That must have been hard," Matt said to Liz, "but over the years, you've earned your silent but deadly, badass reputation by doing some incredibly brave and violent jobs."

She smiled. "Don't get me wrong, I love what I do, but it

took a long time for me to become comfortable with my relationship with the guys. It was worth the time and patience that went into cultivating those relationships, because right now, I have complete trust and faith in them," Liz said.

"You have done that. The guys all have no questions about your abilities," Franco said.

"I'm beginning to see that having that faith and trust is the only way this works. It's life or death situations. I don't think I realized that at first," Matt said.

"When you first got here, I wasn't sure how to play this. I thought, maybe I can insist they embrace you right off the bat, but I realized it would be better in the long run if you earned respect from the guys on your own merits. You almost jacked that up how many times?" Liz laughed.

"Too many to count," Matt groaned.

"It was a bumpy ride for you, dude. David H. was particularly hard on you," laughed Franco.

"At least we're onto bigger and better things now. We should text Jimmie and set up a meeting with him to get his advice on how to get buy-in, want me to do that?"

"Sure, you can set that up, but I don't think we're ready to share everything with the rest of the Team yet," Liz said, looking to Franco and back to Matt. "I want to make sure we have a more solid plan to tell the Team, so maybe you could set the meeting for a few weeks out? In the meantime, I will work on the budget."

Franco and Matt nodded in agreement.

As with any new start-ups, the budget was the determining factor surrounding all their plans. Once the budget was confirmed, they could really get things off the ground.

Over the next few weeks, Matt and Liz had to do a lot of work on their own for the DMF revamp and HTA.

Sitting down in the now-familiar meeting room, Matt sighed appreciatively as Liz slid him his usual Starbucks order across the table.

"What would I do without you?" Matt said, taking a sip.

"You talking to me or the coffee, Sport?"

Matt shrugged and laughed. "I'm grateful for you both. How have you been?"

"Good. I've been busy and . . ." she trailed off.

"And?" Matt prompted.

"I've been talking to Mo again."

Matt prepared himself for more girl talk, wondering if he was going to see more Liz tears. The first time Liz told him about Mo, her on-again-off-again girlfriend, he had seen a very different side of his typically emotionally distanced friend. Her cold stares turned into a stream of tears right in front of him. Her confusion and hurt showed Matt her vulnerable self.

Matt couldn't say anything before Liz went defensive. "Don't look at me like that, ok?"

Matt held his hands up in surrender. "I'm not looking at you any type of way. All I'm saying is, do those on and off again relationships *ever* work out? I don't know if I've ever seen one that did. Have you thought of moving on?"

"Seriously, come on. Do you think it's easy to meet people with what I, we, do for a living? There aren't a lot of choices for me. Sometimes are harder than others with her," she said.

"That's what you said last time we spoke about her. It's just that I want you to be happy, and I don't see too much of that when you speak about her, that's all," Matt said.

Liz nodded. "It's been good this time. I might even be going to see her soon, if I can start using my PTO," she added with a wink. "How's it going with Red Head, I mean, Amber?"

Matt and Amber had been texting semi-regularly, mostly about when they were going to the gym next. They had been working out together a few times a week, but Matt made sure to keep the conversations about the 'safe' categories. Gym-related things, favorite movies, the weather. He wanted more but knew he had to play it safe.

"As good as it can be considering I can never actually be alone with her," Matt said.

"All in time, Sport. Anyway, what do you have on the agenda to talk about today?"

"I had a great meeting with Anthony, a guy I worked with at Tailgaters. He proposed including all the DMF auto, home, and commercial real estate holdings on the policy."

"Which would also give him a much larger commission I would imagine. But that's cool, we're making history. Henchmen with full medical coverage and life insurance is a first in the industry. That is something to be proud of," Liz said.

"I agree. This kind of blows my mind that we are starting something like this. I can't imagine where it will take us. I'm not going to lie, I'm relieved that hopefully I'll never have to draw a gun on anyone ever again."

"I get that, but of all the things you did as a Henchman, drawing a gun was probably the most successful thing you did. You wasted people like it was nothing. You never hesitated. Have you ever wondered how you did that so flawlessly?"

Matt shook his head. "That is nuts. I'd never shot a gun before either. I've thought about how I was able to do that some, not too much because it hasn't bothered me. I waited for a wave of guilt to hit me and shut me down, but it never happened. I kept hearing in my head, 'kill or be killed.' It was almost too simple," Matt said with a shrug.

"That works for me. I think that each of us comes up with something that makes sense to us. Speaking of keeping up our mental health, you know that I've been seeing a therapist for years. I needed the extra help along the way. I want everyone else to take care of their mental health too."

"I couldn't agree more, but I think these tough guys aren't going to be so keen to see a therapist. How are we *ever* going to get them to see the benefits?"

"I'm thinking that having ongoing support groups is where we need to begin. Getting these groups off the ground is just a matter of semantics," Liz said.

"You're right. We just need to come up with a proper name. In the past, they would debrief on the drive home or go talk to Jimmie. I know you want to step it up more but mentioning taking care of mental health will not fly. No one would come if we called it a support group," Matt responded.

"I agree, but hey, I'm confident it would help others learn how to talk about the trauma they go through on the job. It sure as shit wouldn't hurt." Liz paused while she thoughtfully took a sip of coffee. Her eyes brightened as she swallowed. "I know, instead of a support group, we could call it, Bitch Session."

"I like that," Matt said with a smile, then looking at the time on his phone, he continued, "Are you ready to go meet Jimmie? He just texted and said he's ready to meet with us." Matt knew Jimmie had a knack for working with the tough guys and their egos, so he was looking forward to hearing his strategy for revealing this restructuring to the Team.

"Let's go," Liz said, sitting up.

"Do you think this is a pillow or sitting at the desk talk?" Matt asked as they walked briskly down the hallway.

"He usually saves the chairs for when he's pissed, and I'm not feeling the pissed off vibe. My bet is on the floor pillows," Liz said.

"Please have a seat," Jimmie said, motioning for Matt and Liz to sit on the oversized floor pillows. Liz shot Matt an *I told you so* look. "Would either of you like some tea?"

"Told ya," Liz whispered to Matt. Louder, she said, "I'm ok, no tea for me."

"No tea for me either, Jimmie. But thank you," Matt replied.

Jimmie took a loud slurp of his tea. "So, for the buy-in, Ed and I debated between making a Team-wide announcement or letting the selected leaders know first. With the latter, we figured that would be a better way to get the rest of the Team's buy-in. With them on board, and their support behind us, we would address the whole Team. After weighing out many variables, we are leaning towards letting a select few know."

"I think we all agree that it's probably best to get support slowly and not rush it to make it feel like they're being pressured to engage," Liz said.

"Would you help us pick the right guys?" Matt asked Jimmie.

They came up with five names: Ricky, William, Gabe, Skippy, and David M., not David H. The CM Team would be represented by Jackson, they didn't want them to feel excluded, however the track that they would eventually be on would not include the same type of training. They were going to be more of their own version of HTA that both Jackson and Matt would create.

Franco was not on the list, simply because he was in a category of his own. He had always been head and shoulders above the rest—literally, he was the tallest on the Team—in professionalism and quick thinking. They had other plans to use his expertise in a leadership capacity within the HTA. The strategy was to create an air of elite-ness within the group chosen. After some thoughtful discussions, they decided that there was to be a certain amount of fanfare with each of their selections. The thought behind this philosophy was that by putting the chosen in the spotlight, the others who were not chosen could see that there was something special about the ones who were. The selected guys were already natural leaders, considered the high-ranking Henchmen, and the rest of the Team respected them.

To dive in even deeper, they created a ranking system. This would serve to let the Henchmen know that if they wanted to be promoted and strive to be better, there was incentive to do that. Each of the Top Five would be considered a Five Star and would have a gold star pin to wear on their lapels. The next highest level to be reached beneath the Five Star would be the S Class, with the letter S pins to wear on their lapels. There were only fifteen spots in the S Class, which made it a slim selection process. The other levels in order of rank are Saber, Slalom, and Spike, each with their own unique lapel pin. Along with the ranks and promotions came pay raises and bonuses. There would be semiannual skills tests offered for those who qualified. To qualify, a Henchman's supervisor would have to nominate them. A nomination would be for something extraordinary done on an errand. The Henchman would also have to have completed the HTA and come with a recommendation from their instructor.

"This will be the beginning of our new structure within the Team. It's my hope that the guys will see that there is room for advancement within the Team now. They will see that there are levels to strive for," Matt said.

"I like that there are options for some of them. There will be some on the Team who don't aspire to advance, who are happy right where they are," Jimmie noted.

"We get that. Creating a hierarchy also gives structure to

what was a chaotic, fly-by-the-seat-of-your-pants business practice," Liz added.

"Should I take that comment personally?" Jimmie asked.

"Not necessarily, Unc. We know you did the best with what you had to work with. As we move forward with this, you will have support with a 'manual' to reference instead of constantly running into 'hang on for dear life' situations," Liz said.

"Truly bringing Henchmen into the twenty-first century, making history. Glad to be part of it," Jimmie replied.

"So, how should we tell the new leaders? Should we set up a meeting or something?" Matt asked.

"A meeting, yes, but it needs to be special and memorable, one for the history books. I say we bring them to an elegant, five-star restaurant to impress the importance of the meeting," Liz said.

"You know what would also be cool? We should arrange to use the other guys as security for the event, you know, so they would feel part of it in a way," Matt added.

"I like that idea. I will come along for moral support only, as an observer, not a participant in the discussions. I believe that if you drive the conversation to a place where the newly chosen leaders can leave the meeting feeling like valuable assets within DMF, the overarching message would be that the HTA would benefit all who attended, and in the long run, DMF," Jimmie said.

"I'll take care of letting them know about the dinner and who will be providing the security. I'll put it on the errand board and see how that goes," Liz said.

"I would expect questions. Be prepared to answer them thoughtfully," Jimmie said with a smile.

With the next night agreed upon for the introduction dinner, Liz posted on the errand board immediately following the meeting with Jimmie. Matt watched her rearrange previously scheduled errands to free up the evening for the top five Henchman, along with their own number twos invited as their own personal security. The night's event was labeled, "Dinner's on us, Suit and tie required."

To both Matt and Liz's surprise, there were no questions asked. Instead, it was abnormally quiet in the House the next day. Matt enjoyed being on the inside instead of feeling like an outsider looking in. *First time for everything,* he thought as he walked past anxious looks on the men's faces.

As the Henchmen arrived for the introduction dinner and each ordered a drink, the atmosphere shifted from tension-filled to anticipation about what the dinner was all about. They enjoyed an exquisite meal and some story telling amongst the guys along with a few drinks. There was an unspoken rule that only two drinks would be consumed while on company business, which this very much was. As the plates were being cleared, William finally said to the group, "Let's cut the bullshit now. Tell us what this is really about."

This was the moment Matt had waited for all night. *It's go time.* Matt put his best insurance sales agent hat on and stood up to begin his presentation. His presentation had been tweaked from what he presented to Fowler and Jimmie.

"You're right, William, time to cut the bullshit. I'm sure you've seen Liz, Franco and I meeting regularly. I know there had been rumors in the House about what we were meeting about. This dinner is the perfect moment to explain to you what we have been working on," Matt said.

Liz joined Matt and stood beside him at the front of the table. "We wanted to start with you five specifically, because we see you as leaders in the House and on the Team. What we have worked on is the creation of the first ever Henchman Training Academy, the HTA. I want to make sure your minds don't go to this being a criticism of your skill. This is a new way to have formalized training for all Henchmen, not just you guys," Liz said. She nodded to Franco, who took his cue and stood from where he was sitting at the opposite end of the table.

"We need leaders to share in our enthusiasm. We're excited to share this with the DMF Team as well as with Henchmen from all over the world," Franco said.

Despite William being a bit abrasive, Franco's comments were met with curious and affirming nods by the rest of the group. Matt and Liz also looked at each other, as if to say, *we were right about bringing Franco in, in this capacity*. When Franco spoke, it was clear the groups wanted to know more, not less, which is exactly where they wanted to be.

"We figured out a curriculum that will provide specialty areas, so that you all can work doing what you enjoy most, and not just tag along because no one else could go. We can go over the specifics later," Matt said. "One of the things I'm most proud to offer you is a benefits package. You all know that I used to work in the insurance industry, and that got me thinking how great it would be for all of us to have those types of benefits. DMF will be able to offer health insurance, life insurance, and paid time off, meaning you can get paid while taking a vacation."

There was silence in the room for a few moments. There was a lot of looking around to see what others were thinking. It was difficult to read since they all had developed keen, emotionless faces.

Matt cleared his throat. "I'm sure you guys have a ton of questions, please start asking."

The room remained silent, with lots of looks around the room, a few even to the silent Jimmie. Gabe turned to Jimmie to almost get his permission to speak. Jimmie nodded. Gabe said, "None of us have ever had benefits. I think that part is great news. But this whole academy thing? I think we need to digest that more."

"Thanks Gabe. I welcome any feedback you have. What we really need from you to get it off the ground successfully is your support," Matt said.

Skippy cleared his throat to get the floor. He sat back and said, "Looking back, I have to be honest here and say that I do wish I would have had some guidance when I first started. It really was kind of fucked up that the first day, they just gave me a gun and that was that." They all silently agreed by nodding their heads approvingly. The guys spent a moment reminiscing about how they were all approached by a friend who was already employed at DMF to come work on the Team. "The speech I think we were all given upon recruitment was that we would do security. I know most of us had worked as bouncers or doormen in clubs. This job doesn't even come close to that. The salary and steady work enticed all of them to come work at DMF," Skippy said.

Franco said, "I can't say I'm not intrigued by the idea. We've all kind of been the unspoken leaders on the Team for the past few years, which always felt like a lot of pressure to me, to try to keep everyone in check with no protocol or anything, and with no extra money or even real authority. We had to earn respect, but even then, without a real title we are always questioned. We had nowhere to go, no promotion, and no freedom to do our jobs a different way. This new platform will give us a stronger identity within the company."

"Can I just say one thing here?" William said.

All eyes turned to face William. "Of course, yes. Please go ahead," Jimmie said.

William took a deep breath before he continued, "I don't know about anyone else, but I feel that this whole thing may be seen as self-serving. I mean, we all know that Matt has been an unsafe Henchman in many regards. Is giving him this little project a way to keep him in the loop, to just keep him on when there really is no place for him on the Team? It kind of seems like another special consideration for the golden College Boy, treating him differently than the others who make mistakes."

Oh shit, here it comes. They're never going to let my mistakes go. He looked to see if he needed to respond, and if so, what could possibly be said at this point, but Liz spoke first.

"It could also be seen as the beginning of the new way to do business with Henchmen. What you said is the very point of the HTA. Finding what someone is good at and then helping them be better at it, not sticking them in roles that they don't feel comfortable in," Liz said. William rolled his eyes.

"That is an excellent way to look at it. The deeper meaning of this project is to empower all who participate," Jimmie said.

William slammed a hand on the table and glared at Jimmie. "I never get a straight answer from any of you. I'm really fucking tired of it. Matt's been terrible for the most part, it's like you are always making this a bigger concept. None of you have bothered to look at how his actions have impacted our lives here. If the people in this room don't trust him and don't want to work with him, how are we going to be able to get everyone else to 'buy in,' as you're requesting?"

It was silent for a moment after William's rant, then Franco said, "I get it, William. I'm also hesitant to present the idea to the rest of the Team because we all know change has never been seen positively. For fuck's sake, if there is different bread or peanut butter in the kitchen, they cause a scene. Knowing the right way to present this to the rest of the Team may be the first lesson we get from the HTA."

Jimmie nodded. "That is a great point, Franco, and a great place to start with a first lesson on your leadership skills. I would like to help teach all of you how to prepare for the conversation as you present it to the guys. The first impressions can make it or break it for them. If this goes wrong, it could be years before anyone could erase the negative connection to the HTA. I'm confident that we can come up with just the right words, but we need you all on board. Can we count on you, William?"

All eyes turned back to William. He grunted, "I'm in. But not for College Boy, for the good of the Team."

As the rest of the guys nodded, Liz spoke up about what the next steps were. Their idea was to have the Top Five, the new leadership Team, meet with Jimmie individually over the next week. Some of them had never been in his office for anything other than being reprimanded.

"This will be a fresh start from where we may have been in the past. I am looking forward to meeting with each of you. Are you guys ready to get started?" Jimmie said.

"How do you think that went?" Liz asked as she put the 450SL into drive.

"I think it went well, but I wasn't sure how to answer the question about presenting it to the Team, thank God for Jimmie stepping up on that," Matt said.

"I agree, Jimmie will be perfect for that. It's a relief for me to not have it as a big fucking secret any longer," Liz replied, letting out a sigh.

"Hell yes, I'm glad we can mark this off our to-do list. I guess this was a reminder that no matter how well you think you plan, there will always be things that pop up. Being flexible is key here. Are you still thinking we picked the right guys?" Matt asked.

"One hundred percent yes, these guys are the brightest of

the bunch. I know that William still has doubts about you, saying that crap about the HTA being self-serving, special treatment towards you. He'll just have to get over it. He needs to stop with the 'eat shit and die' look on his face every time you open your mouth," Liz said, laughing.

"Well, that's almost expected of him. I try not to let it bother me, or at least not let him know it bothers me. I'm feeling pretty good about how things went tonight though," Matt added.

"I'm going to send a text out to them to thank them for coming. I want to encourage them to meet up together in the next day or two, to have their own debrief. I think we should give them some time to talk amongst themselves," Liz said.

"Since we decided to have the Top Five tell the rest of the Team, I'd like to have some intel on how it goes down. Is that something you can help with?" Matt asked.

"Oh, I have that figured out. Garrett and I will be keeping our eyes and ears open around the House. Garrett is as stealth as they come when eavesdropping on conversations. I'm curious to see how it's received by the rest of the guys in the House," Liz said.

"Me too," Matt agreed. Garrett was a pro at overhearing conversations in the kitchen since that was where he heard about the incidents to report on, so Matt knew they would get some good intel.

Liz suddenly gasped like she'd just seen a ghost.

"What's wrong?" Matt asked, concerned.

Liz smiled. "Nothing's wrong, sorry for the alarm. I just can't believe I almost forgot to tell you the most exciting part, you're going to love this," Liz said, pausing to take a deep breath. Matt had no clue what she was about to say. "My dad, Uncle Jim, and I decided, since we are going to eventually take the HTA global, you should probably have an understanding of our international clients and business. My dad is going on a trip to Italy soon, and he wants you to return to your Henchman role once more to work security."

"What, you mean it? I would fucking love that. An overseas trip, right now? When do we leave?" Matt asked.

"We're leaving in two weeks. It'll also be good for you to spend some time with my dad and hear what he has to say about the business end of things," Liz said.

"That would be awesome. But will the guys on the Team get pissed and think I'm getting some type of special treatment? I don't want to start anything," Matt said.

"They all get to go on an international trip with him at some point, so that isn't an issue. Thanks for thinking of that, though. By the way, you'll need a passport. I think I remember seeing yours in some boxes that were brought over from your condo a few months back," Liz said.

"First, I didn't know you went through my stuff, but yes, I have one. Where are we going?"

Liz smiled. "Perfect, you will be ready to go then. More to come on the itinerary, Sport."

"This is perfect timing, since Ricky and I had a couple of sessions at the shooting range last week. Just because I got lucky pointing and aiming a gun a couple of times and shooting guns in video games didn't make me a firearms expert. But I will say, I'm feeling more confident now, you know, just in case we run into some trouble overseas," Matt said with a sense of protectiveness in his voice.

"Ok, Sport. I appreciate the sentiment, but we don't go looking for reasons to use our weapons," Liz chuckled.

CHAPTER 5
EVIL IS STILL LURKING

The following day after the Top Five dinner, Garrett requested to meet with Matt and Liz in the kitchen to discuss the gossip he had been privy to.

After the lunch crowd wandered back to their rooms, Matt got a text from Garrett to meet him at table number one, the table reserved for private, *leave us the fuck alone* talks. The Team respected the space the table gave, and, since it was close to the door, it afforded even more room to discuss. Matt had noticed Garrett liked to spend his days mingling in the kitchen with the Team rather than being in his office. Matt and Liz arrived simultaneously but from different directions, giving each other a quizzical look.

"Have a seat, guys. Thanks for coming down to meet me. I wanted to touch base on what the scuttle butt has been around the HTA. Let me jump right in. None of the Top Five seem to know how you fit into this if you aren't going to be teaching. William is pretty unhappy with the fact it looks like you got promoted. To me, it seems like he is just using that as a way to push back on the HTA in general," Garrett said.

"Yeah, they're still really pissed at you. I think it's kind of funny," Liz said then rolled her eyes. "Oh, stop looking at me like that, Sport. They'll get over it."

"Let's hope so. I don't get how this is seen as a promotion. It's like when someone who works out in the field is assigned to desk duty. Working on the HTA has been consuming for us. I'm learning which battles are worth a fight, and which ones aren't," Matt said.

"But Matt, you do have to realize there has been a power shift with this move for you. The Team sees it as you moving up to a higher level, while you see it as being a demotion," Garrett said.

"A demotion because I couldn't cut it as a Henchman. I don't have the natural killer instinct," Matt said.

"Well, I would argue that you do actually have that part down. I'm not sure what you didn't get about being a Henchman, except I feel like you either thought too much about what was supposed to happen, or not enough about what was supposed to happen," Garrett said.

"I think you were trying to be too logical and think about other ways to solve the issue, and you got it all wrong in the process," Liz said,

"All wrong? Thanks. Well, we're on to bigger and better things now, aren't we? Let's hope our next steps of getting the buy in from the Team won't be as challenging," Matt said.

"We need to be strategic with the whole 'buy in' aspect. I was thinking that maybe we could engage with some of the guys on the CM Team, not just only the M&M Team. You know, just to get them to feel included," Garrett said.

"Jackson hasn't formally come up with how the CM side of the HTA will function. But that doesn't mean we can't start to have them be included," Matt said.

They agreed that giving the CM Team more to do would make them feel they were just as important and necessary as the M&M Team. Liz agreed to put the CM Team on the errand board to start running old fashion, traditional, non-violent type errands; things like picking up the printing and t-shirts ordered, overseeing the contractors at Pinky's when Matt and Liz couldn't be there, and assisting in the design of the classes to be offered.

"They will eat that shit up. Probably will be one of the first times they were asked to be helpful in their own right," Garrett said.

Over the next week, each of the Top Five met individually with Jimmie and started informing the rest of the Team about the HTA. So far, William remained the most vocal about the stupidity of the whole project. He had a powerful voice amongst the Team, which was concerning to some. William had gone so far as to have his own meetings, trying to sway others away from their support and curiosity with the HTA. It was suggested by Jimmie to let William speak his mind, and to trust that the rest of the Henchmen would attribute his tirades to his larger-than-life personality.

Matt could sense there was a feeling of excitement and anticipation about what the HTA would look like once it was up and rolling. There was a sense of pride in some of the guys as they were going to be the first to either set it up, or to be part of the creation of the curriculum. The number twos and threes, even though they were not chosen, were talking about the fact that they had insurance, which was huge for most of them. Growing up, most of them had state-sponsored insurance. Matt had not calculated the sense of pride that came with the benefits.

Matt had the Team fill out intake forms. He wanted to create a database of the Team's demographic information: married or not, children, how many years in the field, the job each guy liked the most, among other things. Matt was also going to use the information collected to begin creating the overall ranking of each Henchman. The system was to be a key part of how Henchmen were assigned jobs and pay structure. They would be placed in one of the predetermined categories, most of them being on the Spike level. There was a bet placed by the Henchmen in the House about who would be the first to move up in ranks. David H. was five-to-one odds.

Mornings had become routine for Matt, which he fully embraced. He realized that he liked the structure of having a place to be each day and a schedule to keep. If he didn't go to Pinky's first thing, he and Liz met at 'the table' in the kitchen to touch base on the ever-growing HTA to-do list.

"What's on the agenda this morning, Sport? I hope it's a light load today, I feel like I need a little break," Liz said, yawning and slowly putting her head down on the table.

"Ok sleepyhead, we can make it short. Although, you'd have more energy if you didn't stay up till three in the morning every day talking to your girlfriend," Matt said with a pointed look, but Liz just smiled. "Have you ever investigated the education level of the Team? On the intake forms, I noticed that most of the guys dropped out of high school. I think enrollment in the HTA will give them something to successfully complete. We need to make sure upon graduation from the HTA, they will have a certificate to hang on their walls."

Looking up and giving Matt an 'are you serious' eye roll, Liz said, "The official Henchman application doesn't have a space for *level of education completed.* That was sarcasm if you didn't catch it. We didn't predict their excitement about finishing the HTA and graduating from it. This will instill a sense of accomplishment. Assuming there would be resistance to this new structure was a misstep on our part."

"Yeah, I picked up on that, thanks. This has been strengthening the Team more than any team building exercise could ever do. This has gone smoother than I imagined," Matt said.

"You won't believe what Finn asked me the other day. You know how we talked about having HTA swag? Finn came up to me and asked if he could create the logo. He said they wanted to have an HTA hoodie to wear," Liz said.

"I love it! Like the new HTA apparel. They can contribute then, as well. I was wondering how to incorporate their skill set with everything going on."

Liz's head had dropped back down to the table.

"I can see that coffee isn't going to work with you today, why don't you go back to bed. I can only imagine what kept you up last night," Matt said.

"It was nothing fun, that's for sure. No Mo time. I needed to run a late-night errand for my dad. But thanks, I'm going to take a well-deserved nap," Liz said, patting the back of Matt's head as she left the table.

"Good morning boys! What's with the sour pusses? It's a beautiful day! Look at the glorious sun!" shouted Pinky as Matt, Franco, and David H. made their way to the free weight section of the gym. Matt offered a smile to Pinky, but Franco and David H.'s scowls seemed to deepen.

"Seriously, what the fuck. She needs to drink less caffeine and eat some junk food occasionally. How can anyone be like that this early in the morning?" David H. growled.

"Some days it's worse than others," Matt agreed.

"I can't imagine waking up to that energy every day," Franco added.

"Almost as exhausting as the black cloud that's constantly hanging over my head. Have you guys heard anything about the

OT lately? This shit is getting old. What is this guy still pissed about?" Matt asked them.

Amongst the excitement surrounding the HTA, Matt had also been hearing tidbits of conversations from the other Henchman that word on the street was the threat to Matt had intensified with the creation of the HTA. The rumblings were only hearsay, but it still didn't sit well with him. The inability to escape the dark cloud hanging over his life was becoming exhausting.

David H. paused to add another plate to the bench press, while Franco took a sip of water, as if to almost avoid answering. "It's old for us too, dude. He was a pain in the ass way before you got here anyway," David H. said.

"We've heard a couple things from Harry. I guess the OT has been shit talking you all over the place on the Dark Web. Harry has been trying to squash it, since it sounds like it's complete bullshit. But we could confirm one fact from the psychotic ramblings. Apparently, he's fuming about you being elevated to a higher status," Franco explained.

"What the fuck does that mean? A higher status," Matt scoffed. "Does he think I got a promotion? Does he not realize that I was technically demoted? I wasn't good enough to be a full-time Henchman. I guess I'm the only one who feels like I'm an idiot for not being good enough to be an actual Henchman."

"He thinks that you moving into creating the HTA makes you top dog," David H. said. "Isn't that the term we were told?"

"Top dog? I hardly think so. I would sure like to get this guy in a room and explain some things to him," Matt grumbled, taking a plate off to lessen the weight on the bench.

"It seems from what we heard, he feels disrespected, again. It's like he's competing with you, it's creepy as fuck," Franco said.

David H. continued, "Fowler gave us permission to put the

word out that he needs to mind his own business and drop the fucking vendetta already."

"Other than wanting me dead, or out of DMF, what has he, or is he, doing now that's affecting DMF?" Matt asked.

"You can get a better idea about that from Harry, but what I can tell you is that for the CM Team, it's seriously a full-time job to keep him from hacking into the DMF network and crippling it. They feel like idiots by approving him as a potential start up anyway. They're scrambling to try and tighten that up on their end too. Plus having cyber battles with him day and night. The OT is wreaking havoc on their jobs. They don't have time to do much else nowadays," Franco said.

Matt thought it was about time, but didn't say out loud, that DMF seriously upgraded their vetting of new start-ups. Under their old vetting system, the OT had been one of the guys supposedly working for DMF, which was how they had gotten into the incident with the OT pulling the gun. If the OT hadn't been such a poor shot, Matt would have been dead, or at least injured like what happened to Franco. *That's just sloppy work,* he thought.

"Doesn't he have more Henchmen lurking around too? I heard he's trying to turn the other contract tech guys against DMF, so basically, he's just fucking with the CM Team twenty-four-seven," David H. said.

"It makes me feel little guilty that the OT is taking up so much of the CM Team's time. And your guys' time as well, guilty again, feeling like I'm being babysat," Matt said. As soon as the word left his mouth, he was thrown off balance by a shove to the back. Turning around, he saw David H. standing there, fists clenched. Matt gulped; he knew instantly he shouldn't have said that.

"Fuck off, dude. You call us babysitters? Nice, we're here to save your ass, and you can't even say thanks once in a while," David H. spat.

"Shit, that's not how I meant it to sound. It isn't you personally, it's just the situation. I appreciate you being around," Matt stammered. His eyes shifted from the furious David H. to the front desk, where he saw Amber walking by. She literally looked like she was glowing, straight out of a magazine.

"Come on, dude," David H. said with disgust, following Matt's sight line. "Our jobs would be a little easier if you didn't have a gigantic crush on little Miss Redhead."

"Anyway, your protection isn't going away anytime soon. I know you feel like you have a babysitter, but until this guy slows his roll, that's the way it has to be," Franco said.

"Yeah, having you two watching me round the clock isn't good for my image or ego," Matt complained.

"Your image? What image is that? The one where you try to be cool in front of the redhead? I think she's out of your league anyway, College Boy," laughed David H.

"Hey, now watch and learn my friends, watch and learn," Matt said puffing his chest. "And, for your information, I have been invited to travel with Fowler to Italy. I must be doing something right."

"What the fuck, who cares? It's not a big deal to travel as Fowler's security, bro," David H. said.

"And you smooth with the ladies? You teaching us something? I won't hold my breath," Franco laughed.

Over the next few days, Matt grew even more fed up with the constant surveillance on him. He disliked it the most when he was escorted into Pinky's with at least a couple of the guys from the Team. Matt was continually thinking about ways he could impress Amber, but these guys were cramping his style. What little he had.

Just as he was thinking about her, in walked Amber. She made eye contact with him immediately as he was on the bench, about to do a chest press. He sat up and told David H., "Bro, she's coming over here, can you step away for just a second?"

David H., who was watching himself curl huge dumbbells in the mirror, rolled his eyes. "I'll take two steps to the right, but I'm watching you."

Matt didn't have time to respond before Amber set her gym bag at the bench beside Matt.

"How's it going, Matt?" she asked.

"Pretty good. Always better when I see you," Matt said, smiling shyly.

Amber laughed. "Same here." She leaned over to grab a kettlebell bell, turning her eyes to David H. "Who are those guys that come in here with you all the time? It seems like you're never alone. Do they not trust you? Or are they your groupies?"

Putting his head down and letting out a long sigh, Matt answered, "Those guys? They're just some of my coworkers. We all end up going to the gym together, it's just how our schedules work out right now." It was the canned response that he and Liz had come up with ahead of time, with Liz claiming she knew Matt well enough to know he wasn't quite the bull-shitter he needed to be at this point.

"How come you never drive? I see you always getting out of the back seat. You look like some VIP. Are you a VIP, Matt, disguised as a cute, normal guy?" Amber teased. *Did she just call me cute?* Matt hoped his cheeks didn't blush.

"What are you two kids talking about?" Pinky said, bouncing up to them.

Matt said a silent prayer that he didn't have to answer Amber's next question. He and Liz had only practiced the first part of his cover story. He made a mental note to get with Liz and see what he should or could have said instead of turning a dark shade of pink with the flirtatious remark.

Later that day, Matt received a text to meet him in Fowler's office as soon as he could. Getting texts from Fowler were always alarming for Matt. He knew he should stop thinking it was always the worst-case scenario, but the talk about the OT and his ridiculous attempt to look slick with Amber gave him anxiety that settled in his belly.

Upon arrival at Fowler's office, Matt found the door closed. He knew from past interactions that a closed door meant some serious shit was about to go down. Knocking with a light touch, Matt heard Fowler's command to enter.

Matt sat in front of Fowler, unconsciously tapping his foot with nerves.

Fowler said, "I know you've been talking to some of the guys about the little piece of shit, the OT, who has occupied way too much of our time and resources. I wanted to keep you in the loop about what we're doing on the backend about the situation."

Matt nodded. "I'm sick of having this feeling of being babysat all the time."

"Babysat, well, yes, I guess you must feel like that a bit," Fowler chuckled. "Right now, that's the only way to keep you safe. This guy is a real wackadoo. As you know through the CM Team, we have communicated with him on the dark web, whatever the fuck that means. It has become apparent from our limited conversations with him that you have become the object of his obsession."

"That's what I've been hearing. I don't get who this guy is," Matt replied.

Fowler shook his head. "I know, weird as fuck. He has it in his mind that you are my soft spot. That if he could just hurt or even kill you, it would crush me. Don't feel too flattered, you're only the latest crush for him. First it was me, then Jimmie, then Liz."

"Great. I'm an obsession for someone I don't know. I'm not sure how to feel about that." Matt sighed.

"I'm sure it's a little unsettling for you to hear. But know we have your back until this is cleared up. The OT has been posting comments that when he gets to you, it will somehow lead to the demise of DMF. No offense, kid, I like you, but it really won't mean I crumble and lose my mind, or that DMF can't go on without you."

Matt smiled grimly.

"Now, no one had ever laid eyes on the OT until he accidentally shot Franco, at least, we believe that was a confirmed sighting. The guy's an enigma in the cyber security world; he's known by his online presence more than his face. It just isn't the way DMF has ever done business, you meet as men, none of this dark web shit. The OT has made it difficult, if not impossible, for anyone at DMF to get closer to him. This is an alternative way to have a business feud of sorts, not like the old days. Back then, you would meet, hash it out, shake hands and move on. One thing I'm sure of is that whoever the OT is, he's smarter than any other competitor I have ever dealt with. I'm typically not an anxious guy, but we're talking serious amounts of money that could be possibly lost if this asshole can actually infiltrate DMF."

As if on cue, as Fowler finished talking, there was a knock on the door.

"Come in, Jim."

Jimmie entered and laid a comforting hand on Matt's shoulder. "After some thoughtful discussion, we are tightening up your security. This is a precaution and temporary," Jimmie said.

"Franco and David H. already told me," Matt said glumly. "Why does it have to be increased?"

"You didn't tell him?" Jimmie asked, looking in Fowler's direction.

"Shit, no I haven't yet. I wasn't sure we needed to," Fowler said with a bitter note.

"Tell me what?" Matt demanded.

Fowler sighed. "The OT sent me an email recently. I rarely open emails from people I don't know. But the subject line of the particular email caught my attention, 'The Precious Prince of DMF.' Hard to leave that one alone, if you know what I mean."

Matt's stomach did a flip. "What? Am I the Precious Prince of DMF? This asshole is crazy. What does that even mean, how did he get into the DMF server?" Matt asked. Too many questions were going through his mind to process.

"Breathe, Matt," Jimmie soothed. Matt took a deep inhale through the nose and sighed out his mouth.

"I want to read you the email that he sent. It may help, may not, but I don't want to keep anything about this from you," Fowler said.

Dearest Mr. Fowler,

As you know, I have been trying to get your attention for quite some time now. You have repeatedly ignored my attempts to show you all the deficiencies in your network and business model. I am disappointed that you do not see the value I can bring to your company. It literally makes me sick to think that instead of bringing in someone who has skills and knowledge of the industry that could benefit DMF, you chose instead to bring in a complete NOBODY. You treat the Precious Price like he is the savior, and not me. I have to wonder if it is because of his good looks, his stature, or what else could it possibly be? If it is because he saved your life, I could understand it better. But that was pure luck, being in the right place at the right time. The guys I hired that day were idiots, I know that now. I am writing this to tell you I refuse to give up my vengeance. I will not take this lying down. Consider this a threat, unless you notice me, and give me some time and attention, things will just get worse for you, DMF, and the Precious Prince. How are those servers working out for you? Are they as secure as you think?

Fowler finished the email, setting his glasses down on the desk. "Ain't that some crazy shit? I don't want you to worry, though. We're handling it. Isn't that right Jimmie?" he said.

"Absolutely, we have this under control," Jimmie replied.

"How can you say that? This doesn't seem under any sort of control except for his," Matt sputtered.

"Let me explain it this way. We agree he is genius level on the cyber savvy end of the spectrum, but that's a separate issue. What he isn't so genius at is breaking through our Team and knowing how to use Henchmen. He has no one loyal to him. He hires his Henchmen on an as-needed basis. Frankly, the Henchmen he has chosen have been the bottom of the barrel, crap Henchmen. We agree DMF has the upper hand at that end of the spectrum. We know his next moves, we see his patterns, we know how to forecast and be preventative," Jimmie said.

"Does that make you feel any better, Sport?" Liz said. Matt spun around to see her standing near the back of the large office. He hadn't heard her come into the room but was relieved to see her.

"In a way, yes, it does. I guess what you said is true. My options are limited to one thing, and that is to trust the Team to keep me safe. I see why you're giving me an extra set of eyes when I'm out of the House," Matt conceded.

"That's why we thought it would be a good time for you to get a change of scenery by taking on this Italy trip, get your mind off this nonsense. I want you to meet Mr. Fancy Pants Rossi anyway, so this will be a great time to observe this guy," Fowler said.

"I'm grateful for the opportunity to travel with you. I haven't heard much about Fancy Pants Rossi, who is he exactly?"

"He's our Italian counterpart who we are trying to work with putting the NFT deal together. And he is fancy alright. He's got lots of fancy cars and homes," Liz said.

"I look forward to meeting him then. I always admired a quality Italian sports car."

CHAPTER 6
REMODELING

MATT HAD BEEN SPENDING MOST of his days working out and working on the HTA at Pinky's. It was a safe place to be since Pinky had a built-in radar detector and knew everything about everybody. Matt knew that whoever came in, she would know about, and if she didn't, her built-in investigative skills would kick in.

Matt and Liz had decided he needed to be at Pinky's during the remodeling of the two spaces they were going to use as the extension of the HTA. He had set up a little office space at the far end of the front desk near the entrance. Though he was happy to be the on-site manager of this construction project, he would be lying if he didn't admit he had another motive.

Ever since Matt had seen Amber walking into Pinky's, he had been smitten. He had a sappy little smile on his face constantly. He was grateful that he didn't have to make an excuse to go to Pinky's. It was perfect that he had already been working the front desk for Pinky during Amber's initial visit. Now, he was there all the time on official HTA business so no one could say anything. The guys on the Team still razzed him, of course, but how else would he have ever made an excuse to go there every day?

Matt took notice of the time of day when Amber came in. He would look extra sharp on the days she was expected to be there, which ended up being every other day, anytime between seven and eight a.m. He would take more time in the mirror, adding a little extra pomade to his hair and trimming his scruff. Matt had memorized her workout routine. She would always do cardio first, then some lifting. She was usually there an hour to an hour and a half. Matt would sometimes pretend to be enveloped in a tense Zoom business meeting when she came in, thinking it may impress her.

It was nearly eight, and Matt was getting nervous he wouldn't see her when he felt a shadow pass by his desk. Looking up, he saw Amber smiling down at him. "You're going to have to show me what you've been working so hard on over there behind that computer sometime," she said, grinning down at Matt.

Matt smiled sheepishly. "I'm not sure it would interest you much."

"Try me," Amber challenged, crossing her arms over her chest.

Part of Matt wished he could tell her; it would be nice to spill his secret to someone completely outside of the Henchman universe. After a brief silence while he considered it, Matt said, "No." He said it with such a firmness that surprised even him. The light behind Amber's eyes darkened.

"Oh, ok. Sorry I asked," Amber said quickly, starting to walk away.

Matt immediately felt like an asshole. "Amber, wait. I'm sorry, it's just what I'm working on is pretty classified," Matt offered, desperately hoping he hadn't hurt her feelings.

Amber nodded. "I get it," she said, looking at her shoes. "I guess I just wish I knew more about you. Thought maybe knowing your job would be a starting point."

"I want to get to know you more too. Maybe we could . . ." Matt trailed off. Amber's head shot up. This would be the perfect time to ask her on a date, and they both knew the conversation was headed that way. Amber waited for him to continue his sentence with her eyebrows raised expectantly. Matt awkwardly looked anywhere but Amber's hazel eyes. He spotted Pinky lifting a box of t-shirts to hang up behind the front counter. "Um, sorry, Pinky looks like she needs help lifting that box. Gotta go. Bye, Amber."

Matt could've won a speed-walking race with the pace he went to reach Pinky, who was perfectly capable of lifting most any box.

Pinky frowned as Matt approached. "Why are you running away from Amber?"

"I didn't run away," Matt protested, though he did have to catch his breath.

"That's sure what it looked like," Pinky chuckled. "What happened? I thought you liked her?"

Matt sighed, bending down to help Pinky hang the t-shirts up. "I do, that's the problem."

"Just ask her out already then," Pinky said, as if it was the simplest solution. Pinky had been as bad at the guys on the Team, constantly harassing Matt about when he would ask Amber out.

"I don't know if I can?" Matt wondered aloud. How did dating work in his position? Would he have to bring his babysitters on the date? Matt shuddered with embarrassment at the thought.

"Of course you can, all you say is, 'Beautiful Amber, please do me the incredible honor of joining me for coffee.' She'd have to say yes," Pinky said.

Matt shook his head, laughing. "No, it's not the asking her part. I don't know if I'm allowed to date. I'm sure you've heard I'm kind of high-risk at the moment."

Pinky winked. "We'll make it happen, sweetie." She beckoned Liz, who was finishing up a workout of her own, to join them. "It's time for mission 'get Mattie on a date,'" Pinky told Liz.

Liz smiled at Matt, making him blush. "Lucky for you, I could see this coming a mile away and I've already updated Jimmie on the situation. I knew it would eventually lead up to you asking if you could take her out on a date."

"So, can I?" Matt asked.

Liz narrowed her eyes at him. "You really are a lovesick puppy. Yes, you can ask her out, but only to The Vanilla Bean. That's the safest plan we could agree to. That way, you'll still be near, but not all the way alone because Franco, David H., and I will literally be feet away."

Though Matt wasn't thrilled he'd have to be watched the entire time at the coffee shop only a few steps from Pinky's, it was way better to have them watching from nearby than to have his babysitters crash the date. He watched Amber take a swig from her water bottle, heart pounding at the prospect of going out with her.

Pinky smiled and clapped at the news. "Now you've just got to work up the courage to actually ask her on the date."

"Assuming you can get her to say yes," Liz joked, punching Matt's shoulder.

Though he had Amber on the mind, there was a lot going on to distract Matt from his non-existent love life between work on the HTA and preparing for his upcoming Italy trip.

Building the Academy wasn't as easy as they all thought it would be. The contractors blew away almost all the timelines that had been established from the beginning. Contractors. Those flipping contractors. What was it about them that kept them from sticking with a timeline? Matt realized from the start that they had no intention of sticking with the agreed upon date of completion. Some days, there would be a crew of ten men, sometimes only two or three would show up, and other days no one. Being a slave to other people's agendas was never a great place to be. Matt thought about the lessons to be learned from this experience: patience, patience, and patience. He had expressed his frustration with Jimmie as construction 'began.' Matt knew Jimmie, of all people, would have to agree with him and his assessment of the lackadaisical contractors.

The lack of progress became a source of stress and frustration for Matt. So much so that he started to panic and went to a dark place in his psyche. He all but convinced himself that Fowler and Jimmie would pull the plug on the project, blame him personally for the delays, and have yet another reason to fire him from DMF. Matt decided to invite Jimmie to Pinky's to see how the lazy contractors left the remodel, to show him the work schedule he created, and to prove to Jimmie and Fowler how hard he had tried to keep the project moving forward.

As soon as he saw Jimmie walking into Pinky's, his stomach flipped. *Maybe it wasn't such a good idea to show him in person?* Matt's fear of disappointing them consumed him. *Too late now*, Matt thought, *he's already here.*

"Jimmie, thanks for coming. I have been working really long days to get this moving, but how are things supposed to get done with all these delays? I was ready to go!" Matt complained to Jimmie.

"Did you hear yourself Matt? '*I* was ready to go.' That doesn't mean that Dawson Construction was ready. We can use this experience as a lesson in mindfulness. Everything happens the way it is supposed to happen, at just the right time. Irritation, agitation, anger, and frustration are all a waste of your energy. Instead, my suggestion would be to think of other ways to use this time," Jimmie said.

Matt quickly shape-shifted his eye roll into a more thoughtful response to Jimmie's latest philosophical take on all things irritating, gently nodding in agreement. Matt thought to himself, *what the hell is wrong with being irritated occasionally?* That was irritating. Jimmie's responses could be taken the wrong way if a person didn't know him so well. He said things in a way that made life and all its intricacies into teachable moments. It was never like, "Hey dumb shit, what don't you get about stupid lazy contractors? They are *never* in a hurry." Nope, he always made people feel like there was always another way to look at situations, which could lead them to think differently—with a less judgmental and more productive attitude.

"Jesus Jimmie, I don't know if I will ever stop coming to you to get sympathy for a situation, even knowing full well that I won't get it. You're right, I can do other things until they get up to speed. If there is a next time, I had already thought about adding a completion date into the contract with some type of bonus, maybe that would help motivate them," Matt said with some encouragement.

Jimmie smiled back. "Nice reframe, Matt. Life is full of them."

As Matt stood to leave, he hesitated. "Hey Jimmie, I just wanted to say thanks for giving me the chance to get to know Amber more."

Jimmie nodded, looking amused. "Who am I to stop young love?"

Matt smiled nervously. "About that, around when do you think I can ask her out?"

Jimmie's smile widened and he leaned back in his chair. "Soon, Lover Boy."

Matt groaned as he left the office, but he was feeling better. It made him feel a little more connected to the world. Getting out of the House was a good thing, and he sure didn't miss doing the ride-alongs with the guys. Those ended up being a little too stressful for him. The whole carrying a gun at work thing may not be the best fit for him. Matt felt more in his element and was thriving with the creation of the HTA. This side of DMF was definitely more his style. He was grateful that he had something to occupy his time with the increased threat from the OT looming.

The next day, Pinky grabbed Matt on his way out.

"Matt, we have your date with Amber all planned out. Listen closely," Pinky said in an intense whisper. "Jimmie wants to be sure you stay on point with it. Next Tuesday, as Amber is leaving, I'll ask you to run to the coffee shop down the way, all you have to do is ask her to join." Matt nodded and Pinky continued, "We need to take it slow. It won't be you two going out on a fancy dinner date, just a walk down to The Vanilla Bean is all Jimmie would agree to. Now, back to the plan. When I ask you to grab my almond milk latte, she will be headed out anyway. I will say that since you two are leaving together, it would be my treat to buy each of you a coffee. Are you following me?"

"Got it," Matt confirmed. Even though it was meticulously planned out, he'd take what he could get. He was glad Jimmie agreed to it, but he still thought they were being overly cautious. Matt knew they would be proven wrong about Amber.

The following Tuesday, Matt's last day before his Italy trip, he had prepped himself to be ready to follow Pinky's lead on getting Amber to go on their first solo trip. He was sitting at his computer when Amber stopped to say bye on her way out. Before Amber could say anything, Pinky said loudly, "Matt, Darling, would you be a doll and run down to the Bean and grab me the usual? Amber, you may as well go with him too since you're headed out. It's my treat."

"That's sweet of you Pinky, thank you. I would love to walk with Matt to get your coffee," Amber said with a shy smile in Matt's direction.

Matt's palms were sweating, so he shoved them in his pockets. Looking to Pinky, he said, "Remind me what your usual is. An almond milk latte, right?"

"You got it!" Pinky replied with a wink. "Enjoy your little getaway and take your time!"

Matt got up from behind the desk and joined Amber. He held the door open for her.

"That was random. If I didn't know better, I would think it was planned or something," Amber said, taking a step out the door.

Don't panic, she can't know it was planned, can she? "I'm sure she just got a craving for her latte, that's all," Matt said, recovering from a mini panic attack.

As they headed down the mall sidewalk and entered the coffee shop, Matt felt a strange sense of freedom, out with a girl in public. Matt walked slowly to savor the time, and he was pleased that Amber appeared to be in no rush either. Matt was quickly snapped out of the perfect date as he spotted Franco and David H. posted out front of the coffee shop sitting at one of the outdoor tables, Liz in a car out front, and Skippy and his number two, Nathan, following behind them. He planned on ignoring them and hoped Amber wouldn't notice the crowd watching them. He could've sworn he saw Amber's eyes noting each of the sets of eyes watching them, her head on a familiar swivel that he had seen while on an errand.

Trying to salvage the awkward walk, Matt briefly stopped by Franco and David H. before heading inside. "Hey guys, this is Amber, you remember her from Pinky's?"

"How could we forget a face like that?" David H. said from behind dark tinted glasses.

Amber smiled but Matt didn't want to stick around to continue the conversation. *Who is it that they don't trust more, me or her?* As they placed their orders, Matt secretly wished the line had been longer and that it would take a long time for drinks to be made so that he would have a few extra minutes to chat with Amber.

"I seem to never get the chance to ask, how do you like your new place? Are you getting used to living here?" Matt asked.

"You're so sweet to ask," Amber replied, tucking her hair behind her ear. "Yes, I do like my apartment. You know how it is when you move to a new city, you just have to cross your fingers and hope you picked the right neighborhood."

"That's true, just have to go with your gut on things like that," Matt said. "How's your work going? It must be nice to work remotely, no commute would be cool."

"Work is good; yes, no commute is cool, but it's hard to meet new people. Pinky's gym has been a real lifesaver," Amber added. "I notice that there's all that construction going on in the suites adjoining Pinky's. From what I can tell, you have something to do with that. What's being done over there, is she expanding?"

"Oh that, yes, I oversee that. The company I work for ended up buying the whole strip mall. We're remodeling a couple of the empty spaces to use in a different capacity," Matt said proudly.

"That sounds exciting. Must be what you're working on your computer all day, huh? What are the additional spaces going to be used for?" Amber asked, leaning closer like Matt's response would be a secret.

Matt had to think on his feet before answering her question. He didn't want to completely shut it down like he had last time. "I believe they're going to be used as classrooms so some of the guys I work with can take more training classes, stuff like that," he said. He had been coached on how to explain his role at DMF if the subject were to come up. He still needed to get his story straight when it came time to talk about himself.

Just in the nick of time, the barista called to them, saying their coffees were ready. Matt could tell that Amber wanted to stay longer. He wouldn't push it, make a mistake, and not be able to go out with her again, so he hesitantly stood up from the table. He had made a deal with Liz that the first time out solo, he would keep it under fifteen minutes. Amber slowly stood from her seat. They walked over and grabbed their coffees and headed back to Pinky's. Matt was not ready to end the date. It was such a nice, relaxed conversation. He was already thinking about a second date with her, but with the OT still looming, it just may not be safe. As a not-so-subtle reminder, all he had to do was look out to the parking lot where he had killed three guys not too long ago when Matt, Franco, and David H. had been caught off guard leaving Pinky's and Matt was nearly kidnapped. Matt's quick reaction time, killing the kidnappers, was the only reason any of them were still alive. Matt shuddered to think what would have happened to him if the kidnapping attempt had been successful. As they parted ways, both said, 'See you next time,' and awkwardly smiled back at each other.

Matt strolled into Pinky's with a grin only to be interrupted by Pinky saying it was a start, but he needed to get on with it already. She could see a genuine attraction between the two.

CHAPTER 7
FIRST TIME FLYING

MATT WAS FILLED with excitement at the prospect of traveling overseas and being able to discuss business with Fowler. He had so many questions he wanted to ask but had prepared himself to listen foremost. He felt a sense of pride at being asked to travel with Fowler. When Liz told him they were going to Italy, it was even more of a big deal to him. He had never been outside the United States, and Italy was on his bucket list of places he would like to visit one day. He was anxious about impressing Fowler and didn't want to fuck things up and say or do the wrong thing, again. They multiplied his excitement for the trip when he found out they flew private on overseas trips. Being dropped off at the stairs to a private jet and skipping security left Matt feeling like a rock star.

"Take that goofy look off your face dude. It's just a plane ride," Matt heard someone say from behind him on the stairs to the private jet.

Matt snapped out of his daze, and he spotted one of the guys on the CM team. "Hey, I didn't even see you, Jackson. Liz said you were coming. Don't you find this a little bit intimidating?" Matt asked.

"Sorry to disappoint you, but frankly, no, I don't. It has all become normal to me," Jackson replied nonchalantly, plopping into a chair at the far end of the jet while Matt stood, unsure of where to sit.

Matt ducked into the jet, the inside was luxurious, with only ten big leather chairs occupying the space. It felt huge.

Matt heard Liz's laughter coming from the door to the plane. "Aren't you super fucking cool, Jack? When did that happen?" Liz said, joining them and sitting in the first chair on the left. Fowler followed behind her into the jet, and the last member of their group, Max, another guy from the CM Team who looked to be around Fowler's age, came in last.

"Why is he here anyway? What does the CM Team have to do with a meeting with Rossi?" Matt asked Liz.

"We need him here. He understands this NFT stuff better than anyone," Liz said.

"You can ask me why I'm here, you don't have to pretend I'm not and ask Liz. It's not like any one of you could do it," Jackson said.

"Lighten up Jack. He's just trying to figure out who does what," Liz said.

"Sorry dude, I meant no disrespect. I think what you guys bring to the project is important, no doubt," Matt said.

Jackson had already opened his laptop and put in his ear buds, paying no attention to anyone else on the plane.

"Welcome to my world. This is a great way to start the day," Fowler said, smiling at Matt.

"This is quite impressive; I've never flown private. Thank you for asking me along," Matt replied, noticing Liz looking at him over the top of her Ray-ban's. She motioned for Matt to take the seat across from Fowler.

The five rows of two generous seats left Matt with more leg room on a plane than he ever imagined possible. No one else seemed to be phased by the sheer luxury of the oversized leather seats, or the beautiful people serving drinks and making sure the passengers were comfortable. Matt's first thought was how in the hell much this little trip cost, but quickly changed to remind himself this was real. There were people who lived lives like this, and he wanted to get used to it.

As the plane took off and Matt settled in for what would be the longest, but probably most comfortable, flight he had ever been on, Fowler spoke. "We have some time to get into this, Matt. Let's have some food and a couple of drinks."

As if on cue, their first course arrived in front of them. Each course better than the next, Matt was feeling the rock star vibe big time. *I could get used to this.*

After the fifth and final course over a snifter of brandy, Fowler seemed more relaxed than Matt had ever seen him. "So, Matt, I'd like to tell you a little about how DMF Enterprises was created, if you'd like to hear it."

Every head in the jet, aside from Jackson's, turned toward Fowler. Even Liz's interest seemed to be piqued, so Matt knew this was a story he didn't tell often. "I'd love to hear it, sir," Matt said. He noticed Jackson put headphones in and close his eyes.

Fowler cleared his throat and began, "You know, my time in the Army was invaluable for one specific reason, and it wasn't to serve my country. The main objective of my unit was to take things of value from people who otherwise thought their personal property were safe. Meaning that countries, presidents of countries, leaders of foreign countries, business leaders, all were subject to a certain type of theft, in this case cyber theft. Of course, the scale of cyber threats has increased tenfold over the years, which has propelled DMF's growth. A lot of this was possible thanks to this guy here." Fowler nodded his head in Max's direction, who smiled. "Max and I served in the Army together. When I needed to up DMF's cyber game, he was the first call I made."

"Just happy to be here, you old kook," Max laughed.

"So, what really got you into cyber theft as a business?" Matt asked.

Fowler smiled. "Well, while I was in the Army, I remember sitting in the same room as a newly elected president of some small shithole of a country. This guy saw his own financial ruin play out in front of his eyes. To show off how wealthy he was, he logged into his overseas account, basically to show off the staggering amount of money in them. These accounts were filled with money he had diverted from his own country and its people. The timing was perfect. He was bragging about how easy it had been when, all of a sudden, the accounts started to empty. The balances just kept going down and down until there was literally nothing left. It gave me immense pleasure to see this horrible, evil, violent sack of shit lose everything he had stolen from the poorest of the poor of his own country," Fowler said.

"So wait, the U.S. government hacked into all his accounts to steal the money back?" Matt asked.

"I told you, I have been into this shit for years now. The government and its directives are not what the public is told about," Fowler said.

"Pops, you were stealing from him though. Isn't that the pot calling the kettle black?" Liz said.

"No, I wouldn't say that's it," Max interjected. "While in the Army, the unit would 'befriend' dictators like him, devise a plan for his ruin, watch his dynasty crumble, and then be there to help with humanitarian aid and rebuild the country."

"You were working off the same page as Robin Hood then," Matt laughed.

"Yes, a high-level Robin Hood scheme. I took that model with me as I started DMF. It's hiding in plain sight. Basically, identify a target, befriend them, they trust you, you fuck them over, and then you are there to rescue. Not that difficult on paper anyway. Now we are entering into an even more bizarre aspect, NFTs. Liz, can you explain it all to him? I still can't wrap my head around it all," Fowler said.

"I'm not the expert. But what I can tell you is that it's Jackson's job to continue to develop innovative ways to broaden DMF's presence in the cyber-crime network, and this trip required his presence," Liz said.

"Working up how to get the newest NFT project up and running was an enormous undertaking," Fowler said.

Matt causally pulled out one of Jackson's earbuds, and asked, "What do you say, Jackson? Can I count on spending time with you to get the scoop on the NFTs? I know Liz would appreciate it. I have been wanting to spend more time with your CM Team."

Jackson scowled. "Don't touch my buds, bro, keep your hands to yourself. I know that cyber security is big business now. It's what everyone is talking about. I can be a team player and spend some time trying to explain it. The CM team is almost always one step ahead of the next trend in security breaches."

"I would say that's an accurate statement. When I started out, I never could have imagined what type of work DMF would be involved in. The CM Team is really the heart of the company," Fowler said.

"What is the new NFT project about Jack?" Matt asked.

Looking bothered, Jackson sighed, "Look, I'm not getting into the whole project now. But I can share some of what we are doing. We are going to be minting new NFTs to sell at inflated prices. We are going to put them on the market, create a popular NFT chain called Five By One."

"The best part about it, is that when the Henchmen are on an errand, they will also be strongly encouraging the people being paid a visit, purchase these fucking NFTs," Fowler said.

"True they are the heart of DMF, but for now, you know this trip isn't about getting a history lesson from my dad," Liz said, looking to Matt, to Fowler, and back to Matt. "We're here to make his trip safe and secure. There shouldn't be any real concerns, all you will need to do is to follow my lead. Think of how Franco and David H. act with you in public, heads on swivels, that sort of thing," Liz said.

"I trust Liz will show you the ropes as we move through the meetings and bullshit I have to sit through. And, for the record, I am proud of what I have put together in my little home-grown company, ain't that right, Liz?" Fowler said.

"Sure, Pops, you have done a good job, I'm proud of you too."

As they were about to land, Matt sat back looking out the window, feeling grateful for hearing the history of the making of DMF. He had thought little about the inner workings of cyber security, but after spending the last few hours hearing about all the potential ways to generate significant amounts of money, his mind was reeling.

They were staying in the same location where the meeting was to be held, in a magnificent Italian villa that showed its age with the beauty of detailed architecture. The DMF gang were given an entire wing in the villa. The rooms offered were as luxurious as any Matt had ever seen in a movie. Since they were all in one wing, the security was fairly routine as they went directly from the air strip to the villa.

Once they were shown to their rooms, Liz and Matt were to report to Fowler's room. They walked with Fowler directly to the meeting with the Italian connection, Vinicio Rossi. Following Liz's lead, Matt tried to muster up his best death stare on the walk. This was his first time on security for a big meeting like this, but he didn't want anyone to guess that looking at him. He wanted to look the part of an intimidating Henchman.

They stopped outside a pair of beautiful, tall wooden doors. "You two don't need to sit in with me. I'll take Max and Jackson, they speak the same language as the other cyber nerds in there," Fowler said.

"We won't be far, we'll be sitting right outside the door if you need us," Liz said.

"I wouldn't expect anything less," Fowler said, heading into the grand meeting room.

Matt would have rather sat in on the meetings Fowler was attending. Maybe next time, he would be invited in a different capacity.

Standing and keeping his eyes peeled in the empty, wide marble hallway, since Matt wasn't entirely sure of what services he was supposed to provide on this job, he conjured up some mental images of CIA agents with their dark shades on and emotionless faces standing in formations that showed silent but deadly force. Matt asked Liz, "Have I done ok so far?"

"We aren't dead, so yeah, I think you've done just fine. It's not that difficult. Especially things like this, nothing out of the ordinary, a great place for you to observe."

"Perfect, that's what I'll do then. No fuck ups. I'll take my cues from you, is that cool?" Matt asked.

"Sport, that's the only way to play this. You'll be fine. After this, we'll get to enjoy a glass or two of some fine Italian wine. I have to say, I came into this trip on high alert. I wasn't sure, still am not sure, how Pinky set this up. So far so good. What do you think of the Italian Henchmen?"

Matt was surprised by the question. *There is a first time for everything,* he thought. *I've never been asked my opinion on anything job related since I've been here.* "I didn't even notice them now that you ask. Weird. They're around, but they blend in and are not as obvious. They throw off more of a butler or concierge feel. It's still so nuts that Pinky is the international bad ass. I can't always remember that or wrap my head around that. I'm sure she vetted him before making the introductions. She knew this Rossi guy from her sordid past when she lived in Europe?"

"Yes, it's crazy to think about her organizing underground corrupt political coups all over Europe. She is a heavy hitter. Rossi is an interesting guy. I've met him and given him mixed reviews. I'm not sure I trust him, yet. He reminds me of Pinky. They are both chameleons and very intelligent people," Liz said.

"I trust your assessment of him. Would he be a good person to have as a contact with the HTA when we go global and expand to Europe? From what it looks like, he employs a lot of Henchmen. I don't want to get too ahead of myself, but I could see it being a good fit. What does your dad think of him?"

"Slow your roll, Sport. We haven't gotten one class graduated yet. Let's put one foot in front of the other. I'll ask Pinky when we get back about Rossi's level of interest in the HTA. I know she has already told him about it. As for my dad, I think he's just interested in getting the NFT scheme going, his mind's not on sharing the HTA right now," Liz said.

"Got it. I suppose if Rossi isn't a fan, Pinky will be able to come up with someone else who would be willing to partner with us, in the right time." Matt winked.

The trip was quick and mostly uneventful. Fowler only had one meeting planned, they had dinner, a short night's sleep, and they were off again. Matt had barely adjusted to the new time zone before they departed. The only part of Italy he really saw was the airport and the hotel, but he figured that was true of most work trips. Even so, the experience of traveling with Fowler, in whatever capacity, security or business partner, only increased his desire to immerse himself in the DMF Henchman culture. He had been wanting to be more involved with the CM team, now after spending time with Jackson on this trip, there might be more mutual respect.

"Is it cool if I touch base with Jackson once we are back home to try and smooth things over with him?" Matt whispered to Liz while on their flight home.

"I see this trip got your mind working about the inner workings of the CM Team. He's a strange dude, he gets super paranoid if he doesn't have a proper explanation about someone coming to observe his work," Liz said. "I have a feeling once you hang out with the CM Team, you may never want to come back."

"Yeah, that's so funny, right Liz? I'm a strange dude? How about I just take my security job seriously. Just because I don't open my insights up to just anybody doesn't make me strange. You of all people should know that," Jackson huffed.

Confused how Jackson was able to overhear their whispered conversation, Matt and Liz looked at each to see who would respond to him.

"Sorry for being insensitive, man. I just got the vibe you didn't want me around. Harry wouldn't even allow me in the CM room until he cleared it with you. I just want to be as well-rounded as I can be," Matt said.

"I don't like what I have heard about you. But, since you're here to stay, for the moment, then I guess I'll make accommodations to have you observe what the CM Team does and how we contribute to the overall success of DMF and the HTA. And if you're up to it, we can dive into the NFT scheme," Jackson said.

"Right, yes, the NFTs. I would love to pick your brain and see what your thoughts are on the CM Team's part with the HTA. Right now, I don't know enough about it to include it in the HTA. Ultimately, I would like to offer Henchman with the right credentials to be certified as CM Henchmen too," Matt said.

"There will have to be an incredible amount of background checks to let *anyone* near our networks, but I guess we could talk about a general training for those interested in expanding out to other jobs," Jackson said.

"I think we can get something put together. We'll keep you updated, Jack," Liz said.

Jackson quickly pulled his headphones back over his ears, clearly having surpassed his social limit.

The trip was finally started to hit Matt. Very quickly, he could hardly keep his eyes open. He felt his head slump against the cold plane window. It might have been a dream, but he thought he heard Liz whisper, "Sweet dreams, Sport."

CHAPTER 8
COFFEE DATES

MATT STILL COULDN'T GET over the feeling of walking off a private jet into black SUVs waiting for their arrival. *A life of crime does pay,* he thought. He was finding it hard to stay humble about the rock star travel accommodations. He wanted to brag about this to his friends from The Basement, but it really wasn't something to share, not at the moment anyway. The quick trip to meet Rossi helped Matt feel more connected to DMF and their actual business side of things, not just the Henchmen side of DMF. His life was now filled with excitement, first class travel, international business connections. This was way more than he could have ever imagined way back when in his past life, daydreaming out his office window at Tailgaters Insurance.

Since returning from Italy, Matt had to work extra hard to keep up with the HTA work. To his pleasure, Amber had noticed his absence and this time, she asked him to grab a coffee with her to catch up. It had started becoming routine.

The weeks had started to blend together. Matt would wake up, go to Pinky's to work out with Franco and David H., shower at the gym, go with Amber to get coffee, meet with the contractors, then work on HTA curriculum and planning.

At Matt and Liz's next progress meeting, they began as usual, talking about girls before getting to business.

"How have your dates with Amber been going? That first date must have gone well to lead to an almost daily walk to The Vanilla Bean," Liz said.

Matt and Amber had started going for coffee after most of her trips to the gym. The trips had progressed to sitting and talking to each other for longer than fifteen minutes, but Matt was still instructed to keep it under an hour each time. The talks were surface level with not much substance, but they did the trick in keeping Matt keen on spending as much time with her as possible.

"It's been really good. I've been learning a lot about her. Like, her favorite movie is the *Kill Bill* series, but she likes volume one the best. To be honest, I hadn't known any girls who've said that was their favorite film, but she told me she's a big martial arts fan, so that makes sense," Matt gushed. Amber had also told him that she was an only child whose parents died in a car crash years ago, but he didn't want to share her personal story with Liz. He was able to talk to Amber about his own family, which was nice because he hadn't been able to talk much about his family since he'd been here, whom he missed, so getting to tell stories of what it was like to have brothers and sisters like he did was a nice trip down memory lane.

Liz smiled. "I can tell you really like her, Mr. Smooches."

"Not you too," Matt groaned. Not only did he have to endure making small talk with Amber day after day, but he also had become the brunt of the Team's relentless jokes about being a lovesick puppy dog. The razzing Matt took was first class, including a new nickname of Mr. Smooches. "You know David H. actually called me that in front of her yesterday while he was making kissing motions?"

"It will only get worse when you ask them to stop. I bet you feel like you are back in your awkward middle school years," Liz joked.

"Hey, I know one thing this has taught me is I am going to enroll myself in the 'How to Bullshit a Bullshitter' course at the HTA. I really need to learn how to hide emotions on my face and at least learn to not blush so badly in front of beautiful girls," Matt said.

After another coffee date with Amber, Matt was sitting at his usual spot at the front desk at Pinky's when she waltzed her way up to him with a dreamy look in her eye. "You two are sure cute together. I love watching young couples start off. It's a sweet thing to be part of," Pinky said, sipping her latte.

"I'm not sure where this is going, Pinky, but it's nice to go out with a girl, even with me feeling like I'm being eyeballed the whole time," Matt said.

"Those boys are just trying to keep you safe, Sweetie. Don't be ungrateful for that, it isn't a good look on you. When is the real date happening?" Pinky asked.

"If it were up to me, I would have asked her already. But there are a few people who seem to think Amber's the devil in disguise. Until I can prove them wrong, I have to sit around and wait for approval," Matt said.

Liz, who Matt noticed had been watching, walked up to the desk. "You know that will take a bit to plan. There are some things we are not comfortable with, as far as her story goes."

"What do you mean? Not comfortable with what exactly? I know I need to get permission to see her for anything more than a cup of coffee, but things are progressing for us. Walking to the coffee shop won't be enough pretty soon," Matt said. He had his sights set on asking her to dinner but knew Jimmie would have to approve the date along with setting up the security needed to ensure Matt's continued safety.

"We're working on it, Sport. I don't want to get into the details with you right now. No one wants to kill your love life, but business is business," Liz replied.

"You sure about that?" Matt asked. "I know you think I'm a nerd and that a beautiful girl wouldn't be interested in me."

"That's not it at all, Sport. In our world, people with no past are dangerous, plain and simple. Something about her feels off to both Jimmie and me. Jimmie just thinks it's a little too neat, a little too normal, which is not normal. Of course, I think you can land any hottie you want," Liz said.

"Ok, but as of now, neither of you have found anything bad about Amber despite all your efforts and digging," Matt said.

"I know, on paper she looks harmless. She may be who she says she is, but don't forget the OT is anything but predictable. Being extra cautious about anyone entering your life was the best way to keep you and DMF safe," Liz said.

"I understand that. I've heard this for months. But how much organizing would it take for me to go out on a proper date with her?"

Liz sighed. "I was going to wait for Jimmie to tell you the good news. I don't think he will mind if I tell you first."

"Really? About going out on a real date? Dude, I am so pumped about this."

"You owe me for this. They were super reluctant about it until I talked them into it. We will set the plan in motion like it was a regular job."

"I wouldn't expect anything less from you and the Team. I really do appreciate it. Can I ask you another favor?" Matt asked Liz.

Turning her head in a questioning gesture, she said, "Ok?"

"I'm not wasting any more time waiting to ask her. I wanted

to give you a heads up to let you know. I don't want to ramp up my anxiety even more by hearing your conspiracy theories on Amber. Can you just relax on those for a while? Just give me a break from that. Please," Matt said.

"I suppose I could do that. But for the record, I know I *am* right," Liz huffed.

The next day at Pinky's, Amber finished her workout and was about to leave when Matt hurried to meet her at the door. "Hey Amber, before you go, can I ask you a quick question?"

He had flashbacks to when the last time he asked a girl out: Catherine. He felt a pang of guilt. Catherine was a co-worker from his days at Tailgaters Insurance. Matt had gone way out of his comfort zone and asked her out on a date. It was bad timing since he asked her the day everything went down with Fowler at The Basement. He accidently stood her up for their date.

"Hey, Matt, sure," Amber said, smiling and tucking a strand of auburn hair behind her ear.

Matt's mouth dried up and no noise came out the first time. He cleared his throat and tried again. "Well, see, the thing is, I was wondering if you wanted to have dinner with me sometime. I figured we may have overstayed our welcome at the Bean," he said with a quivering voice.

Amber's smile grew wider. "Took you long enough."

Matt felt his whole body release the tension he hadn't realized he'd had in his shoulders, and he smiled back. "I'm so glad you said yes. Well, wait, was that a yes?"

"It's a yes," Amber laughed.

"Is this Saturday good for you?"

"That would be perfect," she said. "I'm really looking forward to it. Just text me and we can confirm the details."

Matt had a scheduled meeting with Jimmie and Liz as soon as he got back to the House.

"I have the general itinerary here," Jimmie said, holding up a piece of paper. He paused and leaned forward to look Matt in the eye. "I have to preface this. From experience, we know that you have gone off script when trying to impress folks. I cannot stress the importance of you sticking to the script the entire evening. This is a risk, and it is crucial that you follow the script exactly. The evening will be flawless if you do. And as an extra tip, when you pick her up, go to her door and escort her back to the car like a gentleman would do," Jimmie said sternly.

"I get it. I really do. I'm looking forward to coming in here and saying some version of 'I told you so' when nothing happens," Matt said confidently. He was too excited to worry about the 'what ifs' that they were preoccupied with.

Jimmie remained stone-faced at the 'I told you so' comment. In his serious, professional voice, he began, "This Saturday, you will go pick her up at her place around 6:30. You will take her to dinner at La Belle Vita and take her straight home. No funny business, and absolutely no walking into her apartment, got it?"

"The rules are so simple, even you would have a hard time screwing this up," Liz sang. "Don't be an idiot and think with anything other than your brain, no matter how amazing she looks. And don't be spooked that there will be quite a few of us around. Henchman here, Henchman there, Henchman everywhere!"

"I got it. Pick up, have dinner, drop off. No going in the apartment, got it, got it," Matt said.

He was more excited and nervous about this date than any other he had been on. In all honesty, he had not been on too many dates in his life; he wasn't the type to date around and before Amber, he hadn't met too many girls he liked enough to ask on a date. With his lack of experience, it gave him even more reason to be nervous. At least he knew Amber, which made it easier. It wasn't a blind date or anything terrifying like that. The chatting at the coffee shop and the gym left Matt feeling like he already knew her.

———

Matt got back to his room to find Liz sitting on his bed, pillows on the headboard propping her up so she could watch the TV.

"Hey Sport, I thought you could use some company, and the usual," Liz said.

"How did you know? This is fucking perfect, pizza, beer, and some Netflix."

"I didn't hear you mention having your best friend here, thanks," Liz sighed.

"Sorry, of course you being here makes it perfect over anything else. Thanks for trying to calm me down. Those stupid fucking contractors are really doing a number on my schedule. I just don't understand work ethic like that, just do your job already!" Matt shouted, pacing the small space around his bed.

"I know it's frustrating for you. Remember what I asked you to do the first night we met?" Liz asked.

"Not really, that night was a blur. What was it?" Matt said, thinking of his first surreal night in the House.

"I told you to chill the fuck out. I'm going to remind you to do that again here with this situation. No one is holding you personally accountable for their crappy work ethic," Liz said.

Matt let out a long sigh. "Ok, if you say so. I'll try the constant gentle pressure on them, and see if that works, because getting pissed at them does nothing but slow them down more."

"I know you must have your date with *her* on your mind as well. I'd give you the same advice for that too, chill the fuck out. Jimmie has things set, and all you have to do is follow his plan. I know you'll be able to do that, right?" Liz asked.

"I'm planning on following it to a T. I can't wait to come back and do a little happy dance and say I told you so. She's just a cool chick that has a thing for me," Matt said, smiling.

"Ok, Sport. I hope that's what happens too. We're all on stand-by in the unlikely event that she turns out to be the OT's cousin or some shit."

As Saturday rolled around, Matt became more confident in the plan for the evening. He had decided to ignore the Henchmen who would be discreetly floating around while he was having dinner with Amber. He stopped by Jimmie's office on his way out, knocking on the door. Jimmie called for him to come in. Matt saw Liz was already sitting in his office.

"Jimmie, thank you for making this happen. I won't screw this up. I'm sure I'll want to see her again, so this will be flawless," Matt said, then smiled sheepishly. "To be honest, I can't wait until tomorrow morning when I come down for coffee and you guys will have to apologize to me about your crazy paranoia about her. Jesus, I feel like half the reason I want to go out on this date so bad is to gloat!"

"I look forward to seeing you gloat," Jimmie said, looking at Liz.

"Fingers crossed on this, Sport. We have your back either way," Liz said.

"I'm headed out now. Wish me luck," Matt said before

grabbing the keys for his new favorite car in the black Audi R8. He was stoked when he saw this new set of amazing wheels in the parking lot. Sliding in the magnificent automobile, he couldn't remember the last time he was in a car alone.

He arrived at her apartment and dutifully walked up to her door instead of sitting in the car and texting her to let her know he had arrived as he had for past dates. She answered the door in an incredibly sexy, black, form-fitting dress that left very little to the imagination.

Stumbling over his words, Matt said, "You look amazing. Wow. Incredible."

Amber gave a coy look as if to say, 'you're fucking right I do.' "Thank you, Matt, you are so sweet. You look fantastic too."

Matt had to shake his head to snap him out of his trance. "I guess we should get going. I made reservations for us at La Belle Vita," Matt said, walking up to the R8.

"Are you serious?" Amber exclaimed, stopping in her tracks.

"I thought you said you liked Italian food?" Matt asked, worrying that he'd made an error already.

"What? No, Italian is fine, it's this car. What the fuck kind of work did you say you did? This is, like, a $150,000 car. Impressive is an understatement," Amber said, smiling and running her hand over the hood.

"One of the perks of my job, I guess. Not anything I take for granted. I always dreamed of driving cars like this. To clarify, this is a company car, not mine," Matt replied. He couldn't hide his grin as he held the car door open for her.

"Either way, it's a dream car that you get to drive around. And, for the record, I love Italian food, so points for you on choosing that," she said, settling into the passenger seat.

The rest of the drive to La Belle Vita was filled with an

awkward silence. Matt wanted to save all the safe, pre-planned small talk for dinner. As Matt and Amber were shown to their table, he caught a glimpse of Jimmie sitting in a dark corner table. They were not seated in the general vicinity of his table, but he was close enough that Matt felt like he was being babysat. At least the restaurant was quaint and dark enough that he could be inconspicuous.

The cozy Italian dinner was going according to plan, on both ends. Amber did appear a little on edge and distracted, but Matt thought maybe she was just nervous. She spent most of the night looking over her shoulder. She kept turning her head often enough that Matt felt like he had to say something.

"Are you expecting someone else to come? Your head has been on a swivel most of the evening," Matt said.

Amber blushed at the question and locked eyes with Matt. "What? No, who would I be looking for, silly? I may be a little distracted, that's all. I have this weird sense that we're being watched. It's creeping me out, I think that's why I keep looking around. It's not that I'm bored with your company, if that's what you're thinking," Amber answered with a smile.

"Being watched? No, I can't say I feel that," Matt said, even though he knew a third of the restaurant was filled with DMF Henchmen. "But, I have had a little too much to drink, so maybe I'm not thinking clearly." That second part was true at least. They'd finished the first bottle of wine surprisingly quickly, with Amber acting as the good host and making sure his glass was never empty.

"Speaking of drinking," Amber said, gesturing for their waiter to come to the table. "Could we please get another bottle of your finest red? Thank you."

With the alcohol in his system, Matt was feeling more comfortable with Amber. He trusted her, so, without much thought, he leaned closer to her. "I bet you're wondering how a nice guy like me got mixed up in a business like this," Matt said in a lowered voice, feeling paranoid about Jimmie listening. Matt was getting a little tipsy, which always made him talk more than usual. Until now, Matt had not been able to tell his story to anyone. The urge to process this was something that was gnawing at him. He had not perfected the shoving down of traumatic events as the other Henchmen had.

"Sort of, yes, I do. But I'm still not sure what 'business' you're in exactly, and how your company can afford to have a car like that," Amber replied. He could tell her full attention had been turned on him.

"I can only share so much, but let's start with DMF."

"DMF?"

"That's the company I work for."

"Security company, right?" she asked with her eyes narrowed and her gaze past his shoulder.

Matt laughed. "Security, yeah, pretty much. We have some important people we take care of. And to be honest, I wasn't looking for a job when all this happened. I used to sell insurance. Can you believe that?" Matt said, taking another long drink of red wine.

"Insurance, interesting. So, how do you go from insurance to security and working in a gym?" Amber asked, leaning in closer. Her face was only inches from Matt's, and she blinked her long eyelashes at him and cocked her head to the side.

The words tumbled from his mouth. "I've had too much wine, but what the hell, I suppose it won't hurt to tell you. It's a strange story for sure." Matt paused to take a breath, then continued, "I used to play a lot of video games. I would go to a place called The Basement nearly every night. It was a place where gamers could go drink and play on a network with other guys in the bar. I had a few friends there. Anyway, one night I was there, minding my business, and there was a shootout."

She raised her eyebrows. "A shootout? No kidding! What happened? Tell me more about it," she urged, taking a small sip from her glass.

Matt shuddered, thinking back to that night. "It was really fucked up. One minute I'm playing games with my friends, the next minute I'm crawling on broken glass with gunfire all around me. I was the last one to leave. On my way out—I was so close to the door I could see my truck in the parking lot—I turned around one last time and saw a few men were dead, at least I think they were. That's when I saw a man who was wounded and in terrible shape. I couldn't leave him; I wouldn't have been able to live with myself if I'd done that. It was instinct for me to pull the stranger out of harm's way and to take him to a safe place. That night changed my life," Matt said, looking down at his lap.

Amber gently placed her hand on Matt's arm, sitting in silence. It wasn't the reaction Matt thought he would get. It was as if she felt sorry for him or knew could at least sympathize, like she knew the exact feeling. That look only lasted a moment before her face relaxed into a smile.

"You're so brave, Matty," she said with a sigh. Her words were slightly slurred. "I wish I was as brave as you."

"I don't think I'm brave. I'm just lucky. And you're pretty brave yourself, moving to a new place all by yourself, knowing no one."

"Well, not all by myself. I have my cat with me, who you still need to meet by the way."

"Mr. Big, right?"

Amber smiled widely. "That's his name. You're so attentive, Matty, it's sweet," she said softly, running her hand on his arm. "Let's cheers to our first date. And you've got to finish that glass, I think I've had more of that bottle than you!"

Matt shook his head and smiled as he clinked his glass with

Amber's. With two bottles gone, he could tell that Amber was feeling her drinks, or was she? He couldn't decipher if her words were slightly slurred or if his hearing was muffled. He also couldn't tell if she was being flirtier than usual. It seemed like she was, but was it real, or just perceived in his blurred alcohol stupor? Matty this, and Matty that with her coy smile was enough to distract most.

After finishing his glass, Matt noticed her eyes darting around the restaurant again, seemingly distracted again. Matt wondered why she was still so uneasy, but he fought the urge to call her out and end the date abruptly.

Standing up and bending over with her arms on the table, her chest practically in Matt's face, she said, "Matty, when I get back from the little girl's room, I think we should get out of here."

"Sure, we can leave," Matt said with a quick glance at Jimmie. Once she was gone from the table, Matt wanted to run over to Jimmie and ask him what to do. He had to get a clear head, s*hit, we should not have ordered that second bottle of wine.* Jimmie must have known what Matt was thinking. He completely ignored Matt's pleading look for help out of the situation.

Amber traced her hand along Matt's shoulder when she returned from the bathroom. "The night is young, Matty. It would make me so happy if you could drive us back to my place and at least let me make you a coffee or something. That's kind of our thing, you know? We have coffee together, how it all started," she said, smiling.

"As great as that sounds, I really can't come up to your place tonight. I have an early start tomorrow. I would love to some other time though," Matt said, sounding as monotone as if he were reading the exact script Liz had written.

"That's a shame," she said, jutting out her bottom lip in an exaggerated frown.

The alcohol and longing for companionship coupled with Amber's sexy smile and laugh was a tough combination to ignore. This was going to be difficult to navigate his way out of. As Matt stood up to leave, he nearly fell onto the table. He had not calculated the effect the wine was having on him. Without hesitation, Amber grabbed Matt's arm to steady him, her reaction time not that of someone who was wasted. *Maybe she's not as drunk as she's pretending to be . . .*

"Oh shit, I'm sorry," Matt stuttered. "That wine went to my head, shit. Let me get myself together."

"I think it did me too, I'm a little tipsy, Matty. Driving that fancy car may not be a good idea. Let me call us an Uber, ok?" Amber said. She dug through her purse for her phone.

"I guess so. I'll have to call work and let them know I'm leaving it here then. How embarrassing. The guys will not let me live this one down, I bet. But I also don't want to wreck it, so Uber it is," Matt said.

As they made their way to the front of the restaurant, Amber was the one taking the lead and helping Matt around the table and other customers, making sure that he didn't land face first on anyone's table. As they passed Jimmie's table, Amber swayed, grabbing onto Jimmie's table for balance and giggling as she mumbled an apology. Even through Matt's hazy vision, he could see Jimmie's disapproval.

"I'm really too drunk to drive, I think we should call an Uber to get back to your place," Matt slurred.

"Silly boy, we already decided that, and one is on the way," Amber said.

Matt sighed. "But how am I going to get the car back to the House?"

"Matty, stop. You can call someone to come and get it once

we get to my place. We already talked about that too, so silly," Amber replied.

"Well, that's good, thank you for taking such good care of me," said Matt, leaning down and resting his cheek on the top of Amber's head.

Amber lightly rubbed Matt's back and he felt like he could fall asleep right there.

Amber shook his shoulder once they arrived at her apartment. Matt hardly remembered getting in the Uber, let alone the car ride. Matt remembered the plan and asked the driver to wait, saying he would only be a minute. Despite being quite intoxicated, he still was aware of the deal he made with Jimmie. He would walk her up to her apartment, and not stay. Matt stumbled while walking up to the door. "No more mistakes for me," he said under his breath.

Amber shot him a strange look.

"Sorry, that was supposed to be in my head," Matt mumbled.

As they got to her apartment door, Matt leaned in to give Amber a goodnight kiss, but Amber put a hand on his chest.

"Hey, hold on there, fella. No kisses until you wash up! It will only take a second for you to splash some cold water on your face, and it may sober you up some. I wouldn't want you to not remember our first kiss, it has to be memorable."

"Since you put it like that, then sure, I think it will be ok for me to just go in for a second to wash up, and don't forget our coffee," Matt said, smiling back at her.

"Yes, go in there, big guy. First door on the left. I'll wait for you, right here, for that kiss," Amber shot back in her most innocent voice.

Matt stepped into her apartment. It smelled nice, like vanilla. He continued to the first door on the left and found the bathroom. His swaying appearance in the mirror and droopy eyelids showed him how drunk he actually was. He quickly slapped some water on his face, Amber was right, he needed to sober up. Realizing he had broken Jimmie's number one rule, Matt knew he had to get out of there as quickly as he could. He promised himself he wouldn't get wrapped up in Amber's charms any longer, just a quick goodnight kiss and he was out of there.

Matt opened the bathroom door and before he knew what was coming, strong arms came at him from all angles. He felt a stab in his neck and his knees immediately began to buckle as the world became even more dizzying. With his eyes half open, he glanced up and saw Amber, standing over him in her spectacular dress. She mouthed, *I'm sorry*, before the world turned black.

CHAPTER 9
WTF

When Matt came to, he tried to lift a hand to rub his eyes and realized his arms were bound behind his back. His feet were also tied to the bottom of his chair. Matt briefly opened his eyes, but the bright light in the room immediately blinded him. He had a massive headache: the first sign that he was incredibly hung over. He desperately needed water. Blinking his eyes open again, he discovered the light was coming from fluorescent overhead lights as well as from a small exterior window. He wasn't anywhere he recognized, but it appeared to be some sort of outdated, vacant office building.

Slowly, he pieced together the events leading up to where he was. *Shit, shit, shit.* They kidnapped him, after he broke Jimmie's rule of going into her apartment like an idiot, and Amber was in on it!

Amber . . . His eyes scanned the room, and he didn't see her. He didn't even want to think about Amber right now, all he needed to focus on now was getting out.

He saw two Henchmen sitting in office chairs across from him with their legs kicked up on some abandoned desks, completely zoned out and looking down at their phones. He waited for someone to say something about him being awake as he turned his head to inspect his surroundings, but whoever these Henchmen were didn't notice. Matt thought he could use that to his advantage. Since no one was paying attention to him, he began struggling to free himself from the binds on his hands.

He quickly closed his eyes and went limp when he heard one Henchman say to the other, "Hey, bro, I need a coffee. Probably going to head to Starbs, do you want anything?"

"Iced caramel vanilla latte, and don't forget the whip cream," the other said, not looking up from his phone.

Going to grab a Starbucks on the job? What kind of millennial idiot Henchmen are these guys?

Matt tried to figure out his escape plan. If only he could loosen the rope around his wrists and ankles. It was one versus one now, he could take this caramel vanilla latte guy, couldn't he? Matt knew where he would have his weapon: either in a shoulder holster, an ankle holster, or both. Based on the lack of attention being paid to him, this rookie was more than likely only going to have one in a shoulder holster. Maybe he could surprise him and beat him to his own weapon. He had proven that he was a deadly aim in these types of scenarios. The Henchman looked bigger than Matt, both in size and height, but Matt had been working out a lot at Pinky's lately and he was probably quicker than this beefy guy. Plus, Matt would have the element of surprise on his side.

The Henchman yawned as he kept scrolling on his phone. He pulled some wireless headphones out of his pocket and popped them in, probably watching Netflix. Matt shook his head. He wouldn't even have to fight anyone to get out of here. It seemed like he could just walk out once he figured out how to get untied.

The bonds on his wrists were loosening up as he twisted his arms. Obviously, whoever had bound him was not the best at tying knots. He made a mental note to include a Knot Tying course at the HTA, or better yet, Proper Use of Duct Tape and Zip Ties. Matt finally got one wrist free and could pull the other out. He got to work unwrapping his ankles.

The Henchman still didn't notice as Matt rose to his feet. *This guy has got to be one of the least observant Henchmen ever.* The blood rushed to his head, and he stumbled, feeling dizzy from the combination of the drinks last night, the sedative they shot him up with, and for sitting for who knew how long. He walked around to the office door, but it was locked. Matt turned to look for a key or something to break the handle with when he felt hands on his shoulders.

"Where do you think you're going, punk?" the Henchman asked in a deep voice, sounding more like a growl.

Matt, using his quick reflexes, tried to wrestle the Henchman into a choke hold. Soon, they were both on the ground battling hand-to-hand combat. Matt wished he had already taken this course at the HTA. His head was clear enough to go directly for the holster. The Henchman apparently had the same thought. Both men struggled to get to the gun first. The room was small, which left little room to have a good clean fight without stumbling into the scattered office furniture.

"You're going to pay for this," grunted the Henchman, tossing Matt into one of the abandoned desks.

Matt had one hand in the Henchman's jacket, grasping in vain for the correct location of the butt of the gun. "Not if I get this first, asshole!" shouted Matt.

There was more rolling around, landing on desks, faces being pushed away, punches thrown, when the other Henchman returned with a drink carrier containing two drinks with whipped cream and some scones. "What the fuck, man; how'd he get out?" he yelled as he carefully set the drinks on the desk and jumped into the scuffle.

Two against one, Matt was completely outmatched. The first Henchmen held his arms back while the other threw several punches into Matt's nose. Matt felt the blood dripping down his chin, and he saw stars. One last punch put him right back to sleep.

The next time Matt woke up, it was to someone violently shaking his shoulders. "Wake up, Matt."

Matt's eyes opened, and he tried to put his arms up in defense, only to realize he was once again bound at the wrists and ankles.

"It's just me," Amber said, hands up. "I'm not going to hurt you; I'm trying to help."

He was not in the mood for any more tricks. Matt's head hurt so bad he could puke. More than that, the anxiety-induced nausea he felt from seeing Amber, reminding him of his mistakes, was about to throw him over the edge. Wanting to say something about how she'd betrayed him, he realized that more importantly, he'd betrayed his Team by trusting this complete stranger over his best friend and his mentor. He couldn't believe he'd been so blind. He could feel the shame and embarrassment clinging to him like he was encased in a vacuum sealed bag. He sighed. "I'm a complete idiot."

Amber gently said, "No you aren't. I'm just great at my job."

"Your job? Are you fucking kidding me? You're a Henchman, too? Or Henchwoman, I guess, I don't know what you call it," Matt said.

"I don't have time to explain right now, but yes, I'm a Henchman, and yes, I was sent to you on a job to bring you here, but look Matt, I like you. You aren't the bad guy they told me you were. I'm going to get you out of here."

Matt scowled and shook his head. "So, you work for the OT?"

"OT?" Amber asked.

"Outside threat. The guy who's been threatening me and my family for months?"

"I don't work for anyone," Amber said firmly, crossing her arms. "I'm an Unaffiliated. I just picked up this job online. All I was told was that you were a bad dude, quite the asshole, who needed to be seduced and captured. I started to figure out quickly you aren't the evil person the job described you as. But I've never *not* completed a job."

"Fuck. The one girl I liked ended up only going out with me because she was a Henchman sent to capture me. I will never live this down. Great," Matt mumbled. Not only that, but this girl worked for the OT, the one guy who had an extreme vendetta against him. "I don't know what's worse, the fact that you associate yourself with dipshits like these guys, or that you played me like you did without me even seeing any red flags. I defended you to everyone."

"I promise I'll explain later, but we have to get a move on now. These two assholes ran out to get some food, so we don't have much time. Conversations need to be short and sweet right now. How long were you awake before?"

"Long enough to hear that these guys are stupid as shit," Matt said.

"I agree that these guys are an embarrassment to our profession. I haven't been told what's next from the guy who hired us. Believe me, this is not the way this type of thing usually works. These two numbnuts don't know either. So not cool. But when it comes down to it, they won't be difficult to take."

"Why are you working with these guys then?"

"Like I said, I always finish a job. But I knew I didn't want to let you die at the hands of these idiots. I couldn't break from the plan I was supposed to follow, that would be too obvious, so I had to let you get kidnapped, sorry about that. To catch you up, just so you know, I slipped Jimmie my number and we've been in contact."

"Jimmie?" Matt asked. How had he not noticed her slip something to Jimmie? Because he was shitfaced drunk, he reminded himself.

"I told you I'm good at my job. What I need from you right now is to follow my lead. Trust me, I know what I'm doing," Amber commanded. Her voice sounded entirely different from the sweet, flirty, giggly Amber Matt was used to.

"You're joking, right? I still can't wrap my head around all this, and you're asking me to trust you after you've been lying to me for months? Why should I?" Matt asked.

Amber rolled her eyes. "I already told you why. Look, you don't have to trust me, but clearly Jimmie must trust me since he has known where you are this entire time and hasn't tried to come rescue you or kill me. Besides, what other options do you have?"

Matt sighed. He really didn't have another choice. If he did, his brain was too scrambled to think his way through another option. He had to put his trust in her, and in Jimmie. If Jimmie knew he was alive, then Matt knew he would somehow, someway be rescued.

To see if Amber was a complete lunatic or not, Matt said, "If you've already contacted Jimmie, let me see some proof. Show me the texts, and I'll tell you what I think the deal should be."

Amber pulled the phone out from underneath her bra.

"I was wondering where you put that," Matt said.

"I bet you were. Ok, hold on while this thing turns on. I

knew that paying for these would come in handy," Amber said, pointing to her chest. "They can hold just about anything you need."

The phone made all the normal sounds as the lights came on. Matt knew this was an actual phone and not some prop she was using to trick him. Amber offered him the phone by holding it up close for him to see. There were texts and calls from her to Jimmie's phone. Or was it?

"Take a picture of me, send it to Jimmie, and ask him for a picture back." Matt wanted to know it wasn't some random person with 'Jimmie' as the name linked to a number. "After you take that picture and send it, I want to see Jimmie's response and his picture. That's my deal. Because if he truly knows you're here with me, I doubt you'd walk out of here alive," Matt said sternly.

Amber took the picture of Matt without responding to his demand. She sent it immediately. She looked up at him with tenderness in her eyes.

Their gaze broke when the phone buzzed with a new text. Amber showed Matt the screen. It was Jimmie. His reply was, *Ok? Now what do you want?* and a picture of him flipping her off with his middle finger.

They both laughed slightly as his response, and Matt knew clearly that Jimmie was aware of the situation. Matt knew Jimmie to be strategic and patient, and that he was brilliant in these tension-filled situations.

"What should I say back?" Amber asked.

"Say that you're planning to get me out of here in one piece. And that the training films are helping." Only Jimmie and Liz would know that it was Matt's way of letting them know he was ok, and that he was actively taking part as he was able.

Jimmie texted back with a thumb's up emoji. Matt was

satisfied with the response and felt assured that if it wasn't Amber getting him out of here, then it would be Jimmie.

"Ok, it's my turn to tell you what the deal is," Amber said as she turned the phone off and shoved it back into her bra. "You may not like this next part, but it'll help this move forward and give us both the upper hand. I'm just going to say it, don't get any more pissed at me."

"Jesus, ok, what are you going to do now?"

"I am going to punch you in the face a couple of times."

"Fuck if you are! No way, I've had enough of that shit. No," Matt yelled, trying to scoot his chair back away from her.

"I know it sounds bad, but I need to hit you a few times. It would give me additional credibility with these two assholes. They would be all over it if they saw I took care of things while they were out. Look, I have more experience with this sort of thing. I know how to hit in places that don't hurt as much but cause a lot of blood. It will look way worse than it is. This will make it look like I'm in charge, and that you were getting mouthy, so I took care of it."

Matt sighed. This fucking sucked. He couldn't wait for this shit to be over with. "There's no other way?"

"I think this is the best way. Just go with it, follow my lead. I'm going to rough you up. You're going to bleed but think of that as a good thing. One day, you may thank me for it. Get ready."

Matt closed his eyes.

When the two Henchmen came back with food, they were shocked and a little pleased that the target had just been beaten by a girl. Amber explained that the target had woken from his sleep with a poor attitude and needed to be reminded that he was a POS and had nothing to say. They giggled like little boys.

Matt had never been hit like that by a girl. It was especially strange, too, as Amber kept apologizing for every blow by mouthing *I'm sorry*. His ears were ringing and there was fresh blood running down his face over the old, cakey, dried blood.

Amber waited until after they ate to ask whether the call had been made to the boss, AKA, the OT. One said, "Oh yeah, we tried to call, and he didn't pick up. We were going to try again after we ate." They both stepped out of the room to call their boss while Amber listened in, reporting back to Matt what she was hearing.

Amber's face turned up in disgust. "Apparently, the boss had gotten so caught up in a game he was watching he 'forgot' about this whole situation."

"What's the whole situation?" Matt asked. "You mean me? He forgot I was sitting here captured?"

Amber shushed him and kept listening with her ear pressed to the door. "Oh God, the boss actually asked the Henchman what they thought his next move should be. It sounds like the boss is just as much of an idiot as his Henchmen."

"So, what are they planning to do with me?" Matt asked.

The two Henchmen motioned to have Amber to step outside into the hall and be part of their conversation. They left the door open, and Matt could hear what they were discussing anyway.

"Hey, so, I know you were brought into this job because you're a girl, no offense, but we thought it would be cool to tell the boss what to do with this guy. Trouble is, we can't seem to agree," Henchman One said.

"You think I'm only here because I'm a girl?" Amber said. Matt wished he could see her expression. Based on her tone, he could only guess the disgust.

"I mean, I guess so. I've never worked with a girl before except for when they were Honey Pots. I figured that's what you are too, just a toy to dangle in front of some desperate jerk," Henchman One said.

"Is that what you think? It's a bit more than that, I can assure you. But I'll leave it to you two big guys to figure out what's next. You just promise to give me a heads up. I don't want to mess anything up for you fellas," Amber said.

She came back into the room and rolled her eyes to Matt with a 'you have got to be kidding me' look on her face.

"They're coming back in, be cool," Amber instructed.

"I mean, the easiest thing for us to do would be to just leave him here and tell the boss things are taken care of," Henchman Two said as he opened the door and stepped in, ignoring the fact that Matt could hear them.

"Yeah, I also don't have a problem just shooting him," the other said.

Matt loudly cleared his throat, and they both continued to ignore him.

"Well, the boss wanted some information about the business stuff. Maybe we should just try to get him to talk?" Henchman Two said.

"Yeah, that would make us look good if we called back with some information. Maybe we could end up with a nice, fat bonus too," Henchman One agreed.

Matt almost laughed out loud at the stupidity, and he noticed Amber holding in a laugh as well. She put on her best poker face and told them to go for it. Matt prayed they avoided his face; he was pretty sure he had another concussion.

The two Henchmen began doing some side stretches, turning their heads side to side, and cracking their knuckles. "Let's do this! I love my job!" yelled Henchman One.

They started with a few blows to Matt's abdomen; he took

them fairly well, thanks to his time spent at Pinky's. It was confusing for Matt since they didn't even ask a question or give him a chance to speak. What the hell were they trying to do? Why would you pound on a guy without asking him anything? It was like they forgot what the end goal was, which was to get information to make them look like they had initiative.

After a few blows, Amber pushed her way in and confidently asked what Matt knew about the cyber security within DMF. He honestly hardly knew anything about it and wasn't sure how to answer the question. After a few more blows, the Henchmen started shouting at Matt, "It would do you good to speak up when we ask a question!"

Matt was taking a pretty good beating; he was struggling to breathe. He was certain that earlier his nose had been broken, and now possibly a few ribs were as well. Amber started looking worried.

"Fellas," Amber called, shoving the other Henchmen away. "My turn to ask the questions." She crossed her arms and stood in front of him. "We know *you know* what the next move for DMF's cyber team is. We know Fowler tells you everything. We know you are his pet project, that you have manipulated him into thinking you care about him. We also know that you are only in it for the money, and that you are the one with all the knowledge on this phase of DMF."

This was a strategy that Matt had seen done a couple times before while on errands. He called it the 'hiding in plain sight' tactic. Since these guys were complete tool bags, this was a perfect move. What this involved was basically feeding the target the information they were trying to get out of them. This was used in instances where the questioning was really going nowhere, and it was obvious that the person really doesn't know the answers. It was also to save face, so that as a Henchman, you didn't look like you were completely barking up the wrong tree.

She ended her tirade with a couple of vicious blows to Matt's abdomen.

For effect, Matt gave her a look like he thought she was nuts. The two Henchman were idiots and anything he said, they would believe.

Pretending to spill the beans, Matt said, "Ok, ok, you're right about all of it. I have played the old man like a fiddle. He thinks he's some bad ass, but really, he's a weak old man. He tells me anything I ask about. I have spent all these months getting to know the business inside and out. I know all the plans for the next cyber-security take over. You know some of the details, but I want to be the one who tells the whole story to your boss."

The two Henchmen giggled again like little boys, patting each other on the shoulders and high fiving each other. They ate up Matt's story and couldn't wait to tell their boss.

"Let's take a break from your intense interrogation efforts. Go out in the hall and call him. I can't wait to hear what he has to say. Good work you two," Amber said, rolling her eyes as she turned to face Matt. They were so excited that they rushed to call their boss when Matt finished speaking, congratulating themselves.

"You okay?" Amber asked quietly.

Matt nodded, but he doubted it was convincing.

The Henchmen came back into the room, showing disappointment on their faces. Amber asked, "What's the matter, fellas? Was he not happy with the news?"

"No, it's not that. He didn't pick up again. It's kind of pissing me off. I mean, dude, we're at work here, pick up the phone!" Henchman One complained.

"I'm going to tell him that. He seems like he just doesn't get the entire scene here. He hired us but then only gave us enough information to get this so far. When you get a job, they usually give you the complete package, or they feed it to you step by step," Henchman Two added.

Their boss called back within a couple of minutes. They giggled and answered the call in the hall, leaving the door open for Matt and Amber to hear. They excitedly told him everything that Matt said, but quickly, their faces became confused.

Matt could hear them trying to apologize. Amber took one look at Matt and went to the hall to join the conversation. She took the phone from them.

Amber suggested that they bring Matt to the OT. That way, Matt could talk cyber to him, and he could give away all DMF's secrets. She added Matt may even want to join up with him and leave DMF altogether. "I mean, why would he stay? They haven't even tried to come and rescue him!" Amber said. "Besides, Matt already told us he wanted to be the one to tell the boss. This would be a good time to do that."

Amber nodded to Matt, letting him know the OT was on board.

The "team" gathered their things, cell phones, and chargers. Amber had to nag them to clean up their leftover coffee cups and sandwich wrappers. "Just big dumb children honestly," Amber huffed. "You guys don't want to leave too much evidence lying around here, do you?"

The two Henchmen were still discussing the phone call with their boss and were glad they had pleased him. They were so distracted talking about their triumphant phone call, they almost left without Matt. Amber had to remind them to bring the target with them.

"Oh shit, yeah, that wouldn't have worked so well, not having him!" Henchman One said, laughing.

Henchman Two went over to Matt, pulled out a pocketknife and expertly cut the poorly tied rope from around his ankles and wrists. Matt immediately grabbed for his wrists, rubbing them, trying to get proper feeling and blood flow to them. He wasn't sure what was supposed to happen as they left the building, but he wanted to make sure he was ready to go for whatever Amber or Jimmie had planned. He slowly and gently rubbed his ankles and feet to give himself an extra couple of minutes to assess the situation.

"So, why exactly did you cut the ropes from his wrists? Do you think that's smart? Having his hands free to, I don't know, try to escape?" Amber asked with pure disdain.

"Oh yeah, I guess we shouldn't have done that. Let's use tape this time, I suck at tying knots anyway. Should we tape his feet too?" Henchman One said.

"I would leave the feet unbound unless you want to carry him out," Amber said through gritted teeth.

"Yeah, well, I knew that; I was just messing around!" yelled Henchman One defensively. "Go get that roll of tape from the van!"

Henchman Two quickly turned to leave to grab the tape, when Amber interjected, "If you have had tape this whole time, why didn't you use it? Never mind, I don't really want to know. I'll grab the tape, you guys monitor him while I'm gone, be sure he doesn't move!"

The Henchmen pulled their phones out again the minute Amber left the room. Matt stood there, hands unbound, watching his "captures" play games on their phones. He shook his head.

"For fuck's sake!" Amber exclaimed, walking back into the room a few minutes later without tape. "Who locked the van? Just basic Henchman 101 tip, always leave the fucking door unlocked for a quick getaway."

"Whatever, lady! Like you're some sort of expert," Henchman One snorted, not looking up from his phone.

When she asked for the keys, of course, neither was sure who had them last. Henchman Two thought he had left them in the men's room when he went to use the restroom, setting them on the sink while he washed his hands.

Amber returned with the tape, looking like she wanted to throw it at them. Instead, she walked over and told Matt to put his hands out in front of him. Matt was glad to have them taped in front rather than behind his back. That was not how he would have ever bound a target, but Matt knew these two would never notice, and Amber was being strategic by doing so.

Matt was dizzy as he stood up and Amber forcefully grabbed his arm and led him out of the building.

Amber made sure that Matt walked out first, then the Henchmen, then her. Matt got the sense it was imperative they stayed in that order all the way to the van.

As soon as they got outside, she swiftly took Henchman One's head in her hands and snapped his neck, instantly killing him, all while grabbing his gun from his waistline. She positioned herself to use his body as a shield if needed.

It wasn't necessary; she was quick enough that Henchman Two didn't even get a shot off before Amber squeezed off two shots to his chest. Matt stood silently next to the van, still bound at the wrists. She flawlessly took them both out within seconds. Neither one had a clue that when they walked out the door, that would be the last time they would see the light of day.

Amber quickly threw the gun down to the ground and put her hands in the air to signify her surrender to Jimmie and the Team. The Team appeared out of what seemed like out of nowhere. Matt hadn't seen them until they were standing in front of them.

Franco was there first to immediately take her to the ground. He took her down harder than Matt would have liked, but he also knew there was more adrenaline flowing amongst the Team. Amber was still in the dress from the night before, which seemed so out of place. Franco patted her down, found the cell phone, and nothing else. They put the two Henchmen in the van seconds after they hit the ground. David H. made the call to the CUC, and that was that. Matt's life had come back into focus, too bad his brain didn't have time to catch up.

Scanning the parking lot before they drove off, Matt shuddered to think what could have gone down if Jimmie and the Team weren't there for his rescue. All the vehicles departed except for Gabe's. His assignment was to verify the arrival of the CUC. They put Matt and Amber into the same van. He needed to have some time to process not only her part in this, but what to do with his feelings for her. He didn't have enough energy to do much more than sit upright and keep his eyes open. He knew he looked pretty bad just because of the amount of blood that had dried on his face. His ribs hurt, and it was painful to take a deep breath.

The Team and fleet of vehicles headed to the House. The van with the two dead Henchmen was taken by the CUC to an undisclosed location to never be seen again.

Matt was struggling to take everything in. It happened so fast. In less than a minute, two men were dead, Amber was now a prisoner, he was free, and they were on the way home.

CHAPTER 10
BACK AT THE HOUSE

THE RIDE back to the House was silent and heavy with emotion. It relieved Matt to be out of the imminent danger he had been oppressed by for what had felt so long. He felt a sense of belonging that he hadn't felt since living at the House. The Team had come together, for him. He saw first-hand how powerful the Team could be when working toward the same, well-communicated goal.

But all that happened because he didn't follow the plan. How was he that naive and arrogant? Fleeting thoughts of what could have been drifted in and out of his mind, but none stayed in his exhausted brain. He was looking forward to drifting off to a much-needed rest in his comfortable bed in the House. The drugs the Henchmen had shot him full of still lingered in his system. He was having trouble focusing and distinguishing memories and facts from the hours before. He supposed part of that might be since he drank way too much the night before and hadn't eaten or drank any water since.

Amber was blindfolded immediately after being thrown in the vehicle. The blindfold also shielded Amber from seeing the dirty looks thrown her way by Liz. Matt knew it was going to take a lot more than this for the DMF Team to trust her. No one on the Team had ever earned trust right off the bat. There were many angles she could still play them with, too many questions about her. Was she working for someone else? Matt wasn't clear why she had done what she had done.

Jimmie was the first to break the silence in the van. "Heads up, I want to give an update to everyone. I will be taking Amber to my office alone. We will spend some time chatting and getting to know each other. I am sure you all will be curious about my findings. They will be made available to everyone in good time." Jimmie gave Matt a pointed look.

"No one is better than you, Jimmie. Little Miss Redhead has no idea the treat she's in for," David H. sneered.

"Try not to scare her, David H. Oh wait, she is one of us, can't intimidate her, right Jimmie?" Liz said, kicking Amber's feet.

Liz's kick startled Amber and she jumped in her seat, crouching a bit as if preparing for some type of assault. "It's Amber, by the way. Of course, I'm ready, why wouldn't I be? I'm a professional," Amber said.

"Fuck you," Liz said, reaching out and kicking her in the shins this time.

"Liz, stop," Matt muttered weakly.

Liz rolled her eyes but kept her feet to herself.

"We're all curious about her. I have no doubt she will handle our conversation like the professional she has proved to be," Jimmie said.

Matt had so many thoughts and emotions pulsing in his already aching head. It was going to take a minute for him to sort through everything. Did he feel embarrassed knowing he hadn't listened and had been fooled by her? Did he think Amber had at least partially earned her trust back? Or was he still really upset with her?

The van arrived back at the House sooner than Matt would

have expected. He felt like he had been far away, when really, it was no more than a twenty-minute drive. He was helped out of the van by Franco and Liz, who walked him to the medical suite to be checked out.

The doctor on call was already there. She asked him questions that Matt couldn't answer, like what they shot in his neck, and how long he was out for.

The doctor examined Matt, diagnosing him with severe dehydration and having had a royal ass kicking. Matt's nose was also broken, causing some unflattering colors under his eyes. His ribs were cracked and bruised, but not broken. He was hooked up to an IV to get some much-needed fluids in his body while the doctor sutured large cuts on his face. He felt the all too familiar cloud of fog in his brain.

Hours later, Matt heard a knock on the door of the medical suite. Fowler's head peeked around.

"Matt, welcome back," Fowler said warmly.

"You have no idea how glad I am to be back," Matt replied.

"What's with the dark room?" Fowler asked.

"No lights for now. On top of the mess they made of my face, I have another concussion."

Fowler took a seat in the chair beside Matt's cot. "This is where it all started for the two of us, am I right?" Fowler joked. He inspected Matt's face. "I've seen worse. Nothing some rest and a nice, long, hot shower won't cure."

"I agree, I can't wait for a hot shower and sleep," Matt said.

"Not nice to have your brain scrambled too. Let me assure you, however much time you need to recover is fine, no pressure. Take your time," Fowler said, rising to leave with a two-finger military style salute. He paused in the doorway. "Looks like you have another visitor. Liz, stop by with an update when you are done here."

Matt looked past Liz. "Mr. Fowler, before you go, I just wanted to say, how sorry I am. I know I broke the rules, again. I'm sure that partly why my head hurts. I feel like such a fucking tool."

"Listen kid, I know one thing, we can't let this go. But, just relax for now, get all healed up. We haven't decided what your punishment, or consequences will be. Don't worry about that now." Fowler said.

Liz entered behind her dad and approached Matt's bed. "I will, Pop."

The doctor returned from the next room. "This guy is going to be incredibly sore for the next few days with significant bruising pretty much all over the body," the doctor said. She turned toward Matt. "I'll be here all night in case you need anything. For the next few days, I would suggest a lot of time in bed, but you will also need to get up and move some. Don't overdo it, and don't go to Pinky's until you check back in with me. I would suggest an ice bath here and there to help with the stiffness."

"Thanks, Doc. I will keep my eye on him too," Liz said as the doctor exited to the next room. She took a seat in the chair Fowler had just been in. "How ya doing, Sport?" she asked in a soft tone.

"Feels like I've been punched in the face and ribs a lot," Matt reported. "So, not great, but it could've been worse. I feel worse than I look, I guess."

Liz smiled and patted his shoulder. "You look like shit, so you must feel terrible! I'm glad you made it out in one piece." She paused, then rolled her eyes. "I know you're wondering about Amber. Jimmie asked me to get Amber a change of clothes—code for Jimmie wanting to make his guests comfortable, giving them a false sense of security before his interrogation." Seeing Matt's face, Liz added, "I could smell chamomile tea brewing before I left."

Matt knew Amber was going to be in for a long interrogation with Jimmie. For Amber to stay at the House after the kidnapping, she was going to have to be vetted and vetted again. They had to be sure she wasn't a double agent, only there to infiltrate DMF Enterprises. During the time she was on the job, hired by the crazed cyber-criminal, she had played her parts with such precision. It was clear how dangerous she could be.

"I know you guys have a different opinion of her now, I do too. I trust Jimmie to find out what her agenda is. This is such a fucked-up situation. On one hand, I'm grateful she got me out of the mess, but also, she's why I was in the mess. I was so blinded by her. I feel like a fucking fool. All I kept thinking was how I wanted to come back here and say, 'I told you so.' Now, I can't imagine facing the Team, their jokes and laughs at my expense. I deserve all of it. I'm such an idiot." Matt sighed.

"She definitely had her claws in you. But the guys aren't going to bust your balls on this one. In a twisted sort of way, they were glad they got to work with Jimmie in this capacity. Most of the guys had never seen Jimmie in action like they did. He was all over that shit. I haven't seen him that active in years. The guys learned a lot watching him set the whole thing in motion. So, don't worry about them," Liz said.

"Really? Well, I'd love to hear all the details sometime. I can hardly keep my eyes open right now. I did fuck up again, I didn't follow the plan, so you can say, 'I told you so,'" Matt said with closed eyes.

"I'll hold off on that until you can keep your eyes open long enough for me to see your reaction."

Matt smiled with his eyes still closed. "I don't think I can stay awake much longer."

"I see that, Sport. I'll wait outside if you need anything. We recovered your phone, and I have it right here next to your bed," Liz said gently.

Matt woke some hours later to find Liz pacing the medical suite. "This can't be good," Matt said in a gravelly voice.

Liz wouldn't look at him, and her foot began to tap. "I'm sorry to have to dump this on you now, but I think it's important to have this conversation with you as soon as possible," she said. Turning to Matt, Liz's face grew more serious. "I met with my dad and Jimmie to talk about next steps as far as your status with the HTA. We're finding it hard to keep you in a leadership position with how this all ended up. Consequences for you not following the plan, again."

His chest tightened, his stomach flipping and flopping. He'd never been fired from a job before, but he could only imagine this is what it must feel like. "Consequences, yeah, I figured we would end up having this discussion. Whatever happens, after all the work we put into the HTA, I hope that is still a go."

"The HTA is still happening, but your role has been diminished pretty significantly."

So, am I fired or not? "Diminished how?"

"You are going to be required to enroll in the HTA after the first-class graduates. This is kind of a take-it-or-leave-it offer. The Henchmen you will start with won't know who you are, you will have to start from the beginning, just like them," Liz said.

"Me a student? I will never hear the end of it. I never imagined myself sitting in the classroom. That's so fucking dumb."

"You know what else is fucking dumb, don't you? Do you need me to remind you?" Liz said.

"No, I am quite aware of the situation. I thought maybe the consequence would be something financial, that wouldn't be so obvious to the Team."

"That is the opposite of what needs to happen. They, well, we had to put our plans and lives on hold to come rescue you because you couldn't keep your head out of the clouds. The trust just wasn't there like we all thought it was. Being a student will serve as a reminder of the whole Team concept, one that you are supposedly familiar with," Liz said.

"Yeah, fuck, you're right. I am just embarrassed, I guess. Hell, why not, student it is. I don't want to leave here, yet. You can let them know I will enroll."

"I figured you would agree to the conditions. I think it will help you to learn, but it will also show the rest of the Team that you have been served consequences, essentially being demoted," Liz said

"I get that. And it's becoming obvious to me that I don't get the Henchman way. God, I just want to go back to sleep and pretend this nightmare is over."

"We haven't given up on you, that's the good news. I told them you wouldn't give up on us either and quit," Liz said.

"No, I'm not a quitter, you got that right. I know you had my back in those negotiations, I appreciate that. I plan on graduating with high honors," Matt joked.

"I wouldn't expect anything less," Liz said.

He watched her walk out of the medical suite with a heavy heart. He felt like shit because he had let her down, and because he had never had a friend like her. Liz had helped make him feel at home, and like he was part of something, despite him being unsure of what that was all of the time. *I don't want to disappoint her ever again,* he thought as he drifted off to sleep once again.

Matt woke up in the medical suite groggy and disoriented, like he had been asleep for a very long time. It was dark outside, likely either late at night or very early in the morning. He was surprised to see Jimmie sitting in the chair across the room.

"Oh, hey Jimmie. Man, I'm so out of it, give me a minute to unscramble my head," Matt mumbled.

"Good to see you awake. Take as long as you need, I'm not going anywhere," Jimmie replied. "I brought you some of your favorite ice cream, rocky road. The doctor said it was ok for you to have some." Jimmie offered Matt the pint and a spoon.

Matt gingerly pushed himself up into a more upright position, wincing in pain. "Jesus, I'm really fucking hurting. The ice cream is perfect, thank you so much, for this, and for everything else you did for me. Liz said you put on quite the show for the rest of the guys." Matt dug into the rocky road. "Thank God for that," Matt laughed, then quickly grabbed his ribs. "Oh, shit, that hurts like a motherfucker. Won't be doing that for a while."

"You're welcome. I was just doing what I'm good at. I can whip together this sort of stuff in my sleep. It was good for me to see that I haven't lost my magic touch," Jimmie said with a smile. "You know this isn't the first time I have wrangled together a plan in such a short time. The last time I threw one of these together, it didn't go so well. I learned to make sure all the details were communicated."

"Didn't go so well? What happened, can you tell me?"

Jimmie sighed. "Let's just say that this story is another

reason to get Henchman from all levels trained."

"You have to tell me now; you can't leave this one to my imagination. I'm sure we could use it as a training case at the HTA."

"True, this is another example filled with gaps that led to errors. So, the story. A few years ago, we were to pick up a particular suspect who needed to be asked a few business-related questions, privately. Sounds simple enough, right? Well, not when you have a Team that doesn't pay close attention to the location of the pick-up."

"That would be a significant part of the equation," Matt agreed.

"As it turned out, the Team was tasked to pick up a guy named Joey who worked in the Up and Under Pub's back room. Without writing it down, they went to Joey's Pub instead, which happens to be down the block from the Up and Under. While in Joey's, they got a little too belligerent toward a guy they insisted was the Joey they were to pick up."

"I think I can see where this is going. How many people got hurt that didn't have to?"

"Right, you are following. They made a bloody mess of Joey and his pub while trying to take him. The actual Joey from the Up and Under was warned by some not-so-innocent onlookers. He of course made a quick getaway, while sending some of his men down to take care of the two at Joey's," Jimmie said.

"Too many Joeys on one block," Matt said.

"I had to put together a rescue team to extract our two men. By the time we could get to them, it was too late. They were both gone. It was an unnecessary ending to their careers and lives."

"Sounds like it, what a waste. All because they didn't write down the right place to go. The HTA will help with keeping details like that organized," Matt said.

"Probably a good idea. The primary reason for my visit, other than dropping off the ice cream, was to give you an update on my interrogation of Amber. I want you to know that she is in the House and will stay here indefinitely. I wanted you to know, and be assured that, after my long conversations with her, I feel confident that I have peeled back enough layers so that I have a much better understanding of her. Now that I know who she really is. She has an impressive body of work and is, in my opinion, the most successful Henchman ever," Jimmie said.

Matt raised his eyebrows. "What do you mean most successful? How is that rated exactly?"

"It's subjective; however, she's impeccable in the quality of her work and commands the highest salary of any Henchman, ever. And she is never at a loss for work," Jimmie added.

"Well, if I was going to be played by someone, at least I was played by the best," Matt said.

"That's a good way to look at it. There aren't many who would have been able to stave off her exceptional skills. At some point, we are going to have to talk about your going rogue, again, and not following the plan. I think you probably have some regrets about it."

"Yes, of course I do. I have, 'I told you so' ringing in my ears. I feel like a total asshole. I'm so glad to know that only it was only me that was injured. And Liz told me about my newest assignment, enrolling in the HTA."

"I think you retiring as a Henchman was a good call," Jimmie said, shaking his head. "So, are you ready to hear what Amber shared with me, or do you need to take more time?"

Matt nodded eagerly. "I want to know."

Jimmie leaned forward, face serious. "I started off the interrogation in a non-violent, humble way, asking what her story was, who she really was, and what her end game was at this point. She told me that she had been forewarned about my tactics."

"They are impressive. You don't even know you are being interrogated. You have a hard time keeping your guard up in that Zen den," Matt said.

"She felt the same way, questioning why she felt so at home. She asked what really was in the tea we were drinking. Her exact words were, 'I haven't felt this relaxed in years and I feel like I could stay here forever.'" Matt laughed at that; he could share the sentiment. "Once she settled in, drank some tea, I sat back and simply let her talk. She told me that she was an orphan now and had no loyalties. What she most wanted to talk about was her grandfather."

"Her grandfather?" Matt wondered aloud.

Jimmie nodded. "What a small world it is that we live in. I have heard tales of her grandfather back in the day. I actually met him once. He was a legend. I had great respect for his way of doing business. It was professional, not sloppy," Jimmie said, taking a sip of his tea.

"You knew him? This is a small world, that's just crazy."

"Yes, and from his reputation and what I knew about him, he would have been proud of Amber and her ethics," Jimmie added.

"She held things together that night. Even though she flipped the script, she thought things through," Matt said.

Jimmie relayed that Amber explained she had always been a contract-only kinda girl. She told him about some jobs she pulled, and how fed up she was with the way things were now, with the millennials infiltrating the business. She noted that the complete incompetence was just too much for her. Prior to taking this job, she thought that this job may have been her last for a while. The two Henchmen she was paired with helped her make the decision to be done.

"She said she was anxious because she didn't know what else she would do with her life. She has no other skills and has never done any other type of job. Her grandfather had raised her to be the best in the world, she achieved that, she was the apple of his eye," Jimmie said.

"I guess sometimes you just know it's time for a change, even if you aren't sure what that is. I knew I needed a change and to leave the insurance profession, but I had no idea how to make that happen," Matt said.

"With your past, I know you can understand that. This part I think will be of interest to you especially. She told me she took this job because it sounded easy and quick. This job was the first time she ended up having feelings for the target, that being you. She didn't know how to handle that, and of course had no one to ask for advice. She felt alone for the first time and wished she had a friend. She would see you with Liz, and it touched something inside her. Most jobs don't take this long, and she rarely gets to spend as much time with her target."

Matt's heartrate picked up. "So, do you think this was real? Did you believe her, the part about having feelings?" Matt asked.

"I'm leaning toward it not being total bullshit. I'm not ready to commit one hundred percent. I know she's good, but so am I. She may be truthful in that regard," Jimmie said, smiling.

"I'm not ready to figure all that out now. She beat my ass in that room. She's kinda scary right now. I need more time. My head is still too messed up to take any pleasure in hearing that," Matt said.

"That's smart, I wouldn't expect you to do anything else. There's no rush. Like I said, she'll be here awhile. You have time to figure it out."

Matt nodded. "Tell me about the rescue mission you came up with. I've been hearing it's one for the books."

CHAPTER 11
GETTING UP TO SPEED

Jimmie chuckled. "It may sound ruthless, but I had an amazing time pulling this shit together." He stood up to begin his talk. Pacing the room, he began, "When Amber dropped the note on my table, you didn't even notice because you were plastered drunk. Liz was the only one I told. We both were confused. We didn't know if it was a number to call to hear a ransom request, or what. We decided to not tell anyone because we didn't want to have someone react without proper instruction, and to let things play out. Taking an Uber back to her house made sense at the time. I was hoping that you wouldn't have gone in, but things can change real quick in our business."

They decided that they would call the number and see what response they got. Being proactive in this case felt right. The call was answered by a standard pre-recorded computerized message. They had given her a clue about how to reach them now. The game of cat and mouse had begun at that point.

When Jimmie heard the unedited version of what the guys on the Team saw from the parking lot at Amber's, he became agitated.

"I was pissed with them, could hardly believe they saw the

signs and didn't act on them. Sure, throwing you in the back of the van happened too quickly for them to stop it, but they had a chance to be preventative, and they didn't. Apparently, they noticed, and even commented on the fact that it was a little too convenient that a van was parked right outside her front door, backed in, by the way. They shared with me that they even discussed disabling it somehow, maybe giving it a flat tire. But ultimately, they talked themselves out of that."

Matt sighed. "So much for acting on a gut feeling."

"Agreed." Jimmie continued, "During my discussions with Amber, I pressed her to share where her head was in the aftermath of you being taken. I wanted to use this as a time to put on my bullshit detector. If it sounded too canned, then I would see more red flags."

Jimmie recalled that Amber debated what she would eventually share with him. She made it clear that she wanted to handle the situation her way. On the other hand, she didn't want him coming after her, leaving her unprepared. One thing she was certain about was that she needed him to know that she was on their side, but the game needed to be played by her rules.

Amber ended up sending Jimmie a text. In the text, she said that she wasn't interested in playing her part in this charade any longer, that she would do her best to watch out for Matt to keep him safe, but it had to be her way. The only instructions Amber gave were to wait to be contacted and to be on standby.

"You may be wondering how at the time I was able to let it play out the way I did. Well, she actually dropped a pin with your location soon after your arrival. I listened to my gut on this because anything else would have been reactive and potentially deadly," Jimmie added.

"Your faith in that gut of yours is impressive. I hope that you can figure out how to teach that once the HTA gets going.

We all need to be able to not only tap into that, but to listen to it," Matt said.

"I think this situation just reinforced that belief," Jimmie agreed. "I also questioned her about what she was told about this job when she accepted it. She said that her 'boss' told her that I had ice running through my veins, and that I pretended to be some type of spiritual guru. That I just fed people bullshit, what they wanted to hear to manipulate them, and that I was some militant vegan who wore t-shirts that said things like 'animals don't have free will.'"

"Oh wow. I know she briefly mentioned the crap she was told about me also. Really bad intel, except for the fact that I have seen you wearing that t-shirt," Matt laughed and winced at the same time.

"Yes, in fact I do own that shirt, proud of it by the way. I think you get the gist of what comes next in the story. I got the Team assembled, went to the location, and waited. Waiting was the right call here. Amber said that she had never been nervous about what a target thought of her before."

"I'm the target, right? She cared what I thought about her, interesting," Matt said.

"She wanted to somehow impress on you that despite being a world-class Henchman, you had slowly been disassembling her emotional walls so to speak. Those feelings caught her off guard and were scary and exciting all at the same time."

"I made her feel scared. I'm surprised, but glad to hear that. She scared me too, she worked the hell out of those two Henchmen."

Jimmie nodded. "She added that during the long night waiting, she thought a lot about how her current job's boss conducts business. It certainly wasn't old school. It more resembles a very smart, entitled, greedy fucking millennial who doesn't know shit about the code of conduct. These new guys are playing by their own rules, which no one knows but them. It's hard to follow their logic, as they make up things as they go along. The new generation of criminals see things from a very different perspective. It's no longer like back in the day, heisting shipments, or committing insurance fraud by burning down a business, calling it arson, and collecting a big paycheck. This is a whole new level that is faceless. The mix of old and new was a complete shitshow. She was trained to be old school by her grandfather, but she was the age of millennials."

"Now that you say that, I did notice she was annoyed with the stupidity of the Henchmen on the job that night. She played it off well, but I knew she was way more intelligent than they were. I think we all know now just how intelligent she is. No need to discuss further. But can you update me on the situation with the OT?" Matt asked.

Though Matt rarely saw Jimmie lose patience, Jimmie rolled his eyes.

"In the five days since the extraction, the OT hadn't bothered to contact the two Henchman, although they had not shown up to meet as promised. We had collected both of their phones, but neither had gotten a call or text from him."

Recovering from a rough football game was a piece of cake compared to the ass kicking he received from the two stupid Henchmen and Amber. There were a couple of times when he wondered if he would ever see his bedroom at the DMF house again. This place felt like home now, much more than his own little condo ever did. Maybe it was because he didn't really spend much time in the condo. He was at work, and then The Basement most days. He hurt in so many places that it was difficult to get comfortable, even with the extra pillows Liz brought up for him. The doctor instructed him to keep his visitors to a minimum. One of the few that were on the approved list was Garrett. He was one of the first to stop by his room.

"Dude, you look like shit, but you do look a little better than when they picked you up," Garrett said, sitting on the edge of Matt's bed.

"Yeah, a broken nose is never a good look, but makes for interesting colors under my eyes. I probably feel better than I look. Thanks for stopping by. Anything going on I should know about?"

"Nothing really exciting, I just wanted to get your caught up on a couple things. You know I hear things hanging out in the kitchen. The obvious hot topic is *her*, and the second one is you of course."

"What are they saying about me? I almost hate to ask," Matt said.

"I would say that in general, they are glad that you are *finally* having to serve your time as they say. Entering as a student in the HTA has come with positive reviews across the board, a lot of 'it's about fucking time he gets trained,' etc. is what I've heard the most of."

"I'll take that. At least they don't want me completely gone, or to kick my ass around some more," Matt said, adjusting himself into a more upright position, "What are they saying about her?"

The Henchman are all over the place with their theories about *her*."

"They aren't the only ones," Matt yawned.

"Right, I can't imagine, dude. Some of the Henchmen think maybe she really did come clean; some think she could help nab the OT; some are saying she did only work one job at a time, and she was not loyal to anyone, which helps with the trust factor. The biggest thing Jimmie included in his assessment is that people can and do have the ability to change. Overall, the Team is giving her the benefit of doubt, along with a healthy dose of 'I'm not too sure about you' looks from everyone in the House," Garrett said.

"Benefit of doubt, easy for them, she didn't kick their asses all over the place, emotionally and physically," Matt winced trying to silence a laugh.

"Careful dude, no laughing just yet. Those ribs need time to heal!" Liz said, stepping into Matt's room from the hallway.

"You should see how the Team has responded to Amber walking down the hall in the House. I had to laugh. When they see her approach, they point their two fingers towards their own eyes, quickly pointing their fingers back at her, as if to say, *I am watching you*," Garrett said.

"I'm not going to laugh because it's not funny, it's fucking comical. But my ribs and face don't like to laugh right now. I think it's an appropriate response. How is she taking it?" Matt asked.

"I can tell she wants to say *fuck you* right back. Instead, she is just flashing her coy little smile, casting her magical spell on anyone who will pay attention to her," Liz said.

"I'm an expert on her coy smile and her dark magic," Matt said.

"If I was a nice person, I would bring her to my office and give her some tips on how to navigate her new status in the House," Garrett said.

"What would you tell her? And why would you waste your time with her? She needs to feel like an outcast here, she earned the title," Liz said.

"If I was a nice person, I would try and give her some advice. I'd say that there isn't much she could do to win over their trust, except to walk a fine line, have no time that wasn't accounted for, and, if she was invited to do so, offer her knowledge and insights in forming the classes that would be offered at the HTA. I mean, you can't argue the fact that she is good at her job," Garrett said.

"No shit she's good. But I'm not going to encourage her in any way," Liz sneered.

"Don't forget it was Jimmie who almost insisted that Amber return to the DMF House. Fowler made it crystal clear that Matt's continued safety and wellbeing was a priority of his, which meant it was Jimmie's priority as well," Garrett said.

"I know it was. I'm not on her side right now. That's all I am saying," Liz said.

"Thank you for that. I need to start processing all she put me through before I can form my own opinion of her," Matt said.

Garrett stood to leave. "When you're feeling better, Matt, I have a job for you. Set up a meeting with me soon."

Matt was too out of it to really consider what this job might be. "Sure, Garrett, I'll text you," Matt replied.

Matt was feeling well enough to move from the hospital bed into his room. He was still on bedrest, but at least he was more comfortable.

Matt received a text from Liz early the next morning. He was slowly feeling like himself and seeing Liz would do wonders for his mental health. It would seem like old times. Matt eased himself out of bed with a quick shower, feeling ready to take on the day. He emerged from the bathroom to find Liz sitting on the edge of his bed with a box of donuts and two coffees.

"Good morning, Sport. You're looking well. I thought I

would bring you some breakfast," Liz said, offering Matt a coffee.

"Good morning to you. Thank you for this. Those look amazing. I'm going to have more than one, you can count on that," Matt said.

"Of course, take as many as you want. I got your favorite; did you see the chocolate glazed? I've missed our chats. Your face is looking better, the bruises are not as pretty as they were," Liz said, taking a sip of her coffee. She was talking quicker than normal.

"Thanks, I guess? But for sure, I've missed you too. Nice to feel like things are getting back to normal," Matt laughed, then sighed.

"Cool, so we got that out of the way. Now, I want to update you on my first attempt to make nice with your girlfriend. You don't mind me calling her that, do you?"

Matt smiled and shook his head. "I don't even know how to respond to that. But for now, it's fine."

Liz smiled. "So, you want to hear about the little mind game I played with Amber?"

"Liz," Matt scolded. "Take it easy on her, alright?"

"What? I don't get to mess with her a bit after she almost got my best friend killed?"

Matt shrugged; she had a point. "What'd you do?"

Liz's eyes lit up. "Earlier this morning, when Amber was still asleep, I snuck into her room and just sat and waited for her to wake up."

"Creep," Matt laughed. "How'd Amber react?"

"She was startled but not surprised to see me there. I stared intently, without so much as a blink. I knew she had played this game before and knew just how to play. She said, 'I could play this game all day long, if that's what you need from me.' And you know what? I was the first to blink, not Amber."

"You let someone win? I don't think I've ever seen you give in like that," Matt joked.

"First, I didn't want to waste my time fucking around with her. It was a test to see how she responded and how she handled it. Most Henchmen learn the death stare quickly into their time on the job. It may be something we add on to the curriculum at the HTA."

"That's a skill I still need to learn. That is funny though, I sort of wish I was there to see that go down."

"It was a unique situation for me. She's intriguing," Liz said.

"Don't you go getting a crush on her too," Matt teased.

Liz shoved his shoulder. "You know I'd never. I will say I've never met another me before. All these years, I thought I was the only one who wasn't always used as just a Honey Pot."

"Even before I knew Amber was a Henchman, I thought you'd both get along. It seems like it must be hard in this field to be the only woman surrounded by men. I wondered about that when I first got here. It must be hard for you to not have any friends to talk to," Matt added.

"I guess I got used to being alone, I never realized how it could be with another me here. It hit me when she said, 'Thank you for the clothes and the toothbrush,' that I had never shared clothes with anyone before."

"You brought her clothes?"

Liz nodded. "Let her borrow some to wear when she first got back here. She was in that ridiculous dress she wore on your date. As much as I wanted to kill her myself, I did feel for her having to be here dressed like that. Men can be pigs you know. They were all drooling on themselves looking at her. I told you this already, but you must have been on too many pain pills to remember. I'm still not one hundred percent convinced that she's just not just telling us what we want to hear, that is how good she really is."

"Is she a total psycho killer? How do any of us know if she isn't with the OT? Or what if she herself is the OT?" Matt stammered.

"Relax, Sport, Jimmie has this under control. There is no one better than him to get to the root of a situation. And for the record, I don't think she's the OT. Jimmie told me he's going to ask Amber to help us finally nab that little piece of shit, which we will all be grateful for," Liz replied.

"I don't really think she's the OT, but as we can all see, my judgement isn't on point," Matt said.

"It wouldn't make sense. I think from what I can tell, the story how she became involved with him isn't bullshit," Liz said.

"What are the next steps? I'm not sure how I feel about even seeing her."

"Next steps should be slow. Baby steps, my friend. Know that we have eyes on both of you, every minute," Liz said.

CHAPTER 12
THE VIEWING ROOM

Matt had almost forgot about Garrett's request for a meeting. The thought crossed his mind right before he fell asleep. He sat up, grabbing his phone immediately before his sleep brain forgot again. He texted Garrett to ask about meeting in the morning.

Garrett replied instantaneously. "Can you meet right now?"

As a sort of peace offering, he brought a nice bottle of whiskey with him to their meeting, Matt was hoping that with enough sips of the whiskey Garrett would spill the beans and tell the secrets of behind the scenes of the and all the inner-workings of the DMF House.

"Whiskey, yes! Dude how did you know? I love this stuff," Garrett said, walking to the mini bar in his office. "Can I pour you one as well?"

"Sure, I think I have been cleared to have a couple of sips," Matt said.

Garrett tipped his glass against Matt's. "Cheers my friend, glad to see you on the mend. You heal quick, you seriously looked like shit when they first brought you back. You were not a pretty boy." Garrett laughed.

"I probably felt worse than I looked too. So, tell me about this job you mentioned. I already got kicked out of the HTA planning committee. I now have to enroll as a student. I'm sure you heard that too," Matt said.

"Oh, yes sir, I heard that news. It's not the worst thing, I guess. They could have kicked you out altogether. The job though, yes, I need to run this past you. It has to do with the CCTV," Garrett said.

Matt learned early on that they equipped the House with CCTV, closed caption TV. In the beginning of his internship as a Henchman, he would have one fuck up after another. It seemed like *everyone* knew the instant it happened. It was incredibly awkward and anxiety inducing for him to know there were no secrets in the DMF House.

In the early days at the DMF house, Matt attended a training session with the CM Team, and Matt had coincidently learned the House was literally wired for sound and video. Harry, who was doing his best to keep the OT from taking a deeper dive into the DMF servers and encrypted files, let it slip that the House was equipped with a state-of-the-art closed captioned TV system, and that the OT was quite aware of the system. Speaking about the in-house CCTV was taboo, with no one mentioning it outright in casual conversation. But Matt had always wanted to know more.

"I hardly know anything about the CCTV here, just that it exists. What could I possibly be able to help with?" Matt asked.

Garrett took another sip his crystal bar glass and leaned forward. "I'll let you in on the urban legend of how the House became wired for sound, then we'll get into how you can help. The story goes, years ago, there was some concern that one of the Henchmen was a double agent or some shit. Fowler and Jimmie spent a good amount of time debating how to discover the truth about what was happening with this jerk Henchman. They decided that installing a CCTV system in the House was the only way to go. It didn't take long to catch him making calls to the rival group and feeding them classified information. Since then, it has only been used when unusual circumstances arise. Things like when you showed up with Fowler all shot up and bleeding, or when the mysterious Amber was invited to the House, basically anything that was termed hinky."

"In-case-of-emergency-only type of thing, I get it. But what does this have to do with me?"

"Dude, honestly, I need some help with the hours. I put so much time into it. With your girlfriend here, it's just too much," Garrett said.

Matt cringed at the 'girlfriend' mention. "What do you mean? Hours doing what? I'm not sure I follow."

"When I started here, I was tasked with keeping tabs on the video stream, taking notes on what I observed, and reporting back to Fowler and Jimmie," Garrett said.

"So the videos are watched? You sit there all day and night watching? How is that possible? You must have some help," Matt said.

"I have some help when I need it. But remember, it is not monitored 24/7. Just when needed. The only other Henchman on the Team who knows and helps with it is Franco." Garrett set down his empty glass and walked to the back wall of his office, pushing on one of the massive oak doors.

"I feel like I'm at Redd's with the secret button that unlocks the suit lair," Matt laughed.

"Prepare yourself, it kinda freaks you out the first time you see it," Garrett said. "Here is the DMF *viewing room.*"

Matt stood with his eyes wide. "I have never seen anything like this. It's super fucking creepy and very stalker-ish. The entire wall is monitors! What are there, twelve in total? You can see and hear *everything*."

There was something to watch on all of the screens. One was pointed to the big iron gates at the front of the House, one along each side of the House, with the rest showing any movement in the hallways, kitchen, and some of the bedrooms. Every couple of seconds some of the screens would jump to a new location. The conversations were muted but had the ability to heard when and if needed.

"Jesus, this is not right. There is zero privacy in this place. Just knowing they are always on, seems like it would be a deterrent to anyone trying to pull something unsavory," Matt said.

"I told you it's a lot to take in," Garrett said with a sense of pride.

"If I didn't know you better, I would say you're a nasty pervert, Garrett," Matt said, a little disgusted.

"I know, right! Nasty shit right here! Franco helps, so it takes some of the pressure off me. There are certain red flags we look for or listen for, other than that, it's just on for security purposes and background noise." Garrett pointed to some of the screens. "Dude, look here, the monitors on this wall are on 24/7. Do you see? The gates, and the parking lot, the entrances on both houses. I like that part. We don't want any asshole just walking up in here!"

Matt looked around in the room and wondered if he had ever done anything that would have been considered a red flag. *I mean, I know I was stupid about stuff, but red flags?* He hoped not.

"This is an impressive system, no doubt. Thank you for letting me know, I guess," Matt said.

"Dude, you don't get off that easy, this is where the job I spoke about comes in. There are only four other people who know about this: Franco, Jimmie, Fowler, and me. Jimmie and Fowler don't have time to sit and watch this shit, and Franco and I need a break. So, guess what? Now that you know, it is your duty as a keeper of secrets to volunteer some screen time up here. Sorry dude, that's the way this works," Garrett laughed.

"Can we pretend I didn't see it?" Matt asked. *I never thought this day would come; I actually know something Liz doesn't!*

"Nope, you're one of us now. We even have a secret handshake, me and Franco. Wanna learn it?" Garrett said.

"Sure, I guess, bring it on."

"Ok, here, watch this," Garrett said as he began to position himself. "Put your hand out like we're going to shake hands."

Matt stuck his hand out as instructed. As he offered Garrett his hand, Garrett motioned as if he were to reciprocate and shake Matt's hand, only at the end, he quickly pulled it back and put his hand behind his head as if he were scratching his head. Matt was confused.

"That's it? You have a fake handshake?" Matt asked.

"Well yeah, don't you get it? Whoever reaches out first gets to pull back first. It's like we pretend to shake hands, just like we pretend that we aren't stalkers watching and listening to people. It's like a symbol for that? I thought it was pretty cool, man."

"Got it, thanks, I guess. Now what? Will you send me a schedule or something?" Matt asked.

"Next steps are for you to get with Jimmie. Since Jimmie's pillow talks with *her* are frequent and most times spontaneous, he set up a system for you."

"A system?"

"Yes. To alert you to know whenever she'll be in his office.

Fowler and Jimmie figured that way there would be no secrets. You would be in the loop at the beginning. Just saves time, not having to repeat what story she told that day," Garrett said.

"Ok, well I appreciate the fact that you guys are trying to be transparent about her. It seems sort of like invasion of privacy to eavesdrop though. Never mind, let me rephrase that. Sometimes I forget where I live now. That will work for me," Matt said.

"Good, glad you see the value. Jimmie will send you a text that says, *Look up*. When you see those *Look up* texts, you better drop whatever you are doing and get your ass up here to the viewing room."

Although it was nice to be trusted with the viewing room secret, Matt was experiencing a significant amount of guilt. Since he was a little kid, he'd been terrible at bluffing about a story, and telling a lie was nearly impossible for him. With that knowledge, the next day he avoided Liz. There was not a chance in hell he would be able to look at her without her knowing he was hiding something. He wanted to tell Liz about the viewing room, but Garrett said keeping the secret was a must. Matt and Liz didn't keep things like that from each other. Since Liz was his best friend, he wanted her to know about the room. He was hesitant about telling her, for one, because he was afraid she would kick his ass for keeping a secret like that from her, the other being, that he knew that Liz would never agree to be part of the viewing room team. After some internal debate, he went to Garrett to let him know he was going to let Liz in on the big secret, and that he would cover her shifts.

Garrett just laughed. "Dude, do you actually think she doesn't know? Who do you think helped me to set it up?"

"But you said only four people know! How was I to know that actually five people know?" Matt yelled back.

"Ok, fair point, I thought you understood that Liz is all-knowing. She is the Queen of the castle man. You think Jimmie and Fowler run the joint? Hell no, Liz knows what's up," Garrett replied.

"I knew her voice was respected, but not that much. I guess she will run all of DMF someday. Well shit, that saved me from getting my ass kicked by her for not sharing the secret with her sooner." Matt sighed with relief. *I knew it was too good to be true, Liz does know all, maybe one day...*

Matt's phone buzzed, alerting him of a new text message. His stomach flipped when he read it. *Look Up* was all it said. He didn't look, but he knew it was from Jimmie. He raced to the kitchen before heading to the viewing room.

"Where are you headed in such a hurry, Sport?" Liz said from the reserved table near the back door.

"Hey, I didn't see you there. I'm headed up to, um, Garrett's office, you know what I mean?" Matt said with his eyes trained on the floor.

"Why are you being so weird? I know why you are going up there. I saw *her* going into Jimmie's office a couple minutes ago. I think she's getting a bit addicted to his Zen Den," Liz said.

"Shit, sorry I'm being weird. I'm super nervous about this. It's my first eavesdropping you know," Matt said.

"Yeah, well it could get a little awkward! Better you hear it first-hand. We tried to tell you before, and you thought we were paranoid. Have fun, Sport, let me know how it goes," Liz said.

Matt had already turned to leave. "Thanks, *awkward* is pretty fucking accurate!"

He quickly pushed open the door to the viewing room. All twelve screens were on, showing different areas of the House. Matt's eye scanned them and found the screen he was looking for. There she was, sipping a cup of tea she was holding with both hands. Jimmie's head was tilted to the right as though he was trying hard to be compassionate with her. Matt quickly grabbed the headset and adjusted the volume of screen number nine so he could hear the rest of the conversation.

"I feel like I have a good ten years of my life bottled up inside, Jimmie. Ten years of being a Henchwoman with never speaking a word to anyone about it. It's been so hard to have absolutely no one," Amber said.

Matt was grateful he grabbed a coffee and bagel in case this ended up a long conversation. He settled in the large leather desk chair in the viewing room, putting his feet up on the ottoman.

Amber continued, "I want to make it very clear that I never had a boss or Team behind me. I only took contract jobs. I want to make sure people know I don't have any alliances. I'm off the market, not looking for work anywhere else. I know that some of the Team is suspicious about my motives. I think as we move forward, that is the most important message for me to get across."

"I will be sure to pass that message along to the people who need to hear it. Since you never worked with a Team before, how are you getting used to seeing the same people day in and day out?" Jimmie asked.

Amber let out a wry smile. "That's what I'm finding to be the most difficult to transition from. The second most difficult thing is actually trying to have a relationship with Matt. We had an awkward start, very unconventional. I'm certain that my feelings for him are real. I'm just not sure what is next for us."

Hearing his name, Matt sat up, spilling what was left of his coffee on his lap. *She wants to have a relationship with me? Is that what she said?*

"Matt is a special part of our Team, I guess you figured that out by now. My advice to you on that is to go very slow and not have certain expectations about any type of relationship with him. Keep your feelings to yourself, for now," Jimmie said.

Yes, thank you, Jimmie. I am not ready for any emotional connection with her yet, Matt thought.

"I agree with you. I'll keep my little crush on him to myself. I haven't ever really had it this bad," Amber said, blushing.

"Like I said, keep it between us. Liz doesn't need to know either," Jimmie said.

"The thing is, I've been with plenty of men over the years. In fact, all but one had been part of my jobs. Being with men on jobs led to no real transparency or intimacy. When you aren't even using your real name, and the end game is to take out the target, things like where you grew up, what your favorite movie is never come to the surface," she said.

Jimmie nodded. "I understand. People outside our line of work wouldn't get it."

"The one guy that I had a fling with that wasn't work-related lasted three and a half weeks. It happened during the one and only time I took a vacation. I got in the Maldives after a particularly taxing job. Instead of fighting with the consulate to get a proper visa, I decided to stay. After all, it was a magically beautiful place to be stuck." Amber paused to let out a deep breath and set down her mug. "That's where I met Youssef. I thought he was the most beautiful man I had ever seen. His dark hair and light eyes made him stand out in a crowd in the most rewarding way. He had come to the Maldives for some R and R after a rather successful sale of his import export business. The villa he rented was built so that you had to boat to it, with columns buried in the sand to keep the villa from floating out to sea."

Matt watched as Jimmie continued listening to Amber, only pausing to offer her a fresh cup of tea.

"As our time together was coming to an end," Amber said, "I thought it is too good to be true. I was so out of touch with my emotions because I had such little practice with identifying emotions in general, the thought of leaving him was just too much to bear. I obsessed about how I would be able to leave him and go back to my life as if nothing ever happened. From what I can piece together, that was as close as I had ever come to being in love with someone."

Jimmie let the silence hang for a moment before saying, "Emotions have always been a difficult subject for me as well. I have some compassion for you in that area. I have come to the place in my life where I only tap into them on an as-needed basis. At this point, I think if I began to deeply feel, I may not be able to take it."

"I agree there are no accidents, only fate. It seemed that as soon as I thought about how this would come to an end, it did. Who knows for sure if it was my years of living on instincts, or if it just scared the shit out of me to have my heart start to open, but either way, it ended abruptly," Amber said.

"What happened? Anything in particular, or did you just run off instinct?" Jimmie asked.

"It wasn't a planned move if that's what you are asking. Youssef and I were having a carefree conversation about our favorite movies. I had always loved the movie *Casablanca*. My grandfather had introduced me to the movie, and it had always shared a special place in my heart. As it turns about, Youssef laughed and said, 'Well now, isn't this a small world, that is the city I am from, Casablanca.'"

"I see why you left. I would have had the same reaction. Too good to be true, just came true," Jimmie said.

Matt watched from the viewing room as Amber's face dropped. It seemed to Matt that it was the first time in her life that she had truly had a conversation that was open and transparent. Matt could see the shock on her face, that Jimmie knew what she was feeling in that moment with Youssef. Matt's soft spot for her grew larger as he imagined how confused and disappointed she must have been.

"I knew right there from that moment Youssef claimed to be from Casablanca that it was too good to be true. He was as much a fraud as I was. All I could think about was running away, very quickly. My trained instincts told me to go as fast as I could," Amber said.

"You couldn't distinguish if it was just a coincidence that he was from there, could you?" Jimmie asked.

"Exactly, I packed my bags, shoved my emotions back to where they are safely stored, and left in the middle of the night without a goodbye. Every now and again Youssef creeps back into my mind, but never my heart," Amber said.

"Seems like you have kept that part of you closed ever since those fateful three weeks in the Maldives. That is, until you stumbled upon this incredibly charming naive sweet guy," Jimmie replied with a wink.

Matt shifted in his seat wondering if Jimmie only said that because he knew he was listening. Jimmie was strategic if anything, and Matt knew that he posed that question with intention. He could feel his heart pounding waiting for her to answer.

Amber blushed. "Again, exactly. I don't want to rush anything or put pressure on him. I'll wait until the time is right, when I know he's ready, and I'm ready."

"Of course, if that is the way you want to handle this, I will respect that," Jimmie said.

Matt didn't realize that he hadn't taken a breath since Jimmie asked Amber what her next steps looked like. He took a short inhale and let out a long sigh. He wondered how he would ever be able to decipher her true feelings, and what was for show. He had been the new kid on the block here, he knew how it felt to not have a connection to your past, to leave it all behind. He knew what it felt like to be lonely here, among so many. A phrase that his mom used to say to him popped in his mind, *time heals all things.* Time.

CHAPTER 13
THE INVITATION

WITH THE OT FINALLY CONTAINED, DMF was full steam ahead with putting the finishing touches on the blueprint for the HTA. Matt found solace in getting back to working at Pinky's every day, still overseeing the renovation and construction phase of the Henchman Training Academy.

Now that Amber was not working in her previous capacity, she stuck around the DMF gang without having any other real options. For the foreseeable future, she would stay in the House, which was part of the agreement she made with Jimmie and Fowler. Everyone knew she was there primarily so that DMF could keep their eyes on her.

Proceed with caution. That was the best mantra Matt could come up with. Don't force the issue, just try and maintain a safe distance. Matt had gone to Jimmie to ask what the parameters were with Amber. He didn't want to go in a direction that was not permitted under House rules, or even DMF's rules. Before Amber had spent time on Jimmie's floor pillows, there had been massive amounts of research on her. Jimmie and Fowler had dug deeper than they ever had to find any traces of her past, and perhaps who she really was. It made it a little easier to find out about her after they knew who her grandfather was. That piece of the puzzle helped open more doors to explore who this mystery woman really was.

Jimmie was satisfied enough with her progress, the unpacking of her past, that she was deemed safe enough to be released into the general population of the House. Matt had pretty much stayed away from her until Jimmie gave her the official ok, although running into each other at Pinky's was inevitable. Brief conversations at the gym were approved, as it was in a public place, eyes were watching.

At Pinky's, Amber often tried to say hello to him, but Matt never made eye contact as he mumbled back a short greeting. He didn't know what to say to her. He still hadn't sorted out his feelings. Seeing her in person after the viewing room conversation was awkward enough for him. Trying to make conversation, well, that was just not going to happen. Until on his way out one day, Amber approached him again, looking nervous. "Matt," she called to get his attention.

Matt sighed, looking up and meeting her gaze for the first time in weeks. "Amber," he replied flatly. He wished he had cultivated the dead emotionless stare that the other Henchmen could whip up in nanoseconds. Instead, he felt his face flush and hands begin to shake.

"I just wanted to congratulate you on your progress with the HTA. It's such a creative idea. And so needed in the industry."

"Thanks," Matt said, nodding and looking back down at his feet.

"You know I'm retiring, right?" she asked.

Matt shook his head, glancing back up at her. "Really?"

"Yep, I'm not taking any more Henchman jobs."

"Weren't you, like, the best in the world?" Matt asked.

Amber blushed and this time she broke eye contact. "Well,

I don't know about that. I was good at it, I know that. But now it's time for me to find out what else I'm good at."

"I wish you all the best," Matt said sincerely.

She smiled shyly. "Thank you, Matt. And if you ever have any questions or anything, you know, from the supposed best Henchman in the world, you can always ask."

Matt smiled back. "I will."

One of the unexpected gifts Amber brought with her to the House was her cat, Mr. Big. There had never been an animal in the House until Mr. Big moved in. He was an instant hit with the Henchmen, purring at their feet, and sitting on their laps during meetings or meals. He wasn't Amber's cat any longer, he was the House mascot.

Matt often saw the guys on the Team reach down to scratch Mr. Big's ears or cradle the purring cat like a baby when they thought no one was watching. Maybe Mr. Big could be the House therapy animal as well.

At mealtimes, Matt felt as awkward as he had felt when he was new. Now, it was because he was always trying to avoid Amber. From her very first day, Amber was, unlike Matt had been, offered several seats at each meal. The other Henchman found her beautiful, curious, and, as she was called by many of them, a *sweet piece of ass*.

"Sport, how many tacos are you going to stuff your face with?" Liz asked from across the table at dinner.

"I feel like I'm stress eating. It's so awkward seeing her all the time. Any suggestions?" Matt asked.

"Why don't you focus on the HTA for now. She's not going anywhere. Don't put any pressure on yourself or what the relationship will end up looking like. Keep it casual," Liz suggested.

"I guess you're right. I need to focus on that for now. I know she's not seen as a threat simply because she has no loyalty to anyone, which makes it easier for us to trust her," Matt agreed.

Liz shot Amber a dirty look. "I see she's at Pinky's all the fucking time now. What's your take on that? Do you think she's just chilling there because she's bored, or what? Is she being nosey?"

"She's there almost every day. She told me this morning if I ever had any questions for her about the HTA to ask her," Matt said. Liz rolled her eyes, but Matt clarified, "But not in a bull-shit or flirty sort of way. It is an interesting dynamic from her. I mean, she's one of the best in the world, but she literally has never had a best friend, so she's a little awkward too, which I don't think is an act."

Liz's face softened slightly. "I hate to admit it, but I kind of feel sorry for her. I know my life has not been traditional, at all. But I have always been with family and a Team. I just want to be sure about her agenda."

"I appreciate you keeping an eye out for me. What are your thoughts about officially asking her to be part of the HTA, like offering her a spot there? We can keep her close that way too. She would be a good fit to lead some of the classes," Matt said.

Liz bit her lip thoughtfully. "I want to keep tabs on her, but I also think it would a good place for her. We could use her talent, which she has got a lot of. Plus, it ticks off a box I had," Liz said.

"What box are you referring to?" Matt asked.

"Think about it, Sport, what do she and I have in common?" Liz said with eyebrows raised.

"You're both hot chicks?" Matt laughed.

"Exactly! But seriously, how many of us are there in the field, and how many do we need to have? Lots more than there are. There are more and more high-level businesswomen and

CEOs that don't always want dumb boys hanging out with them all the time. Having an all-women Henchwoman team, oh, what a dream. I could really get into this. I'm outta here, but please add this to the agenda at our next Info-Update meeting with Jimmie and my dad," Liz said on her way out.

During the start-up phase of the HTA, recurring bi-weekly meetings were scheduled. These information-sharing meetings were designed to keep Fowler and Jimmie in the loop about the progress of the construction, budget details, and other miscellaneous events to report.

Would hiring Amber to begin work at the HTA be a good idea or a trap? Matt still wasn't convinced either way. His heart said one thing, his mind another. He was glad he had a Team behind him, to support him and help him work through situations like this. The reality was that the HTA revolved around men, and their place as Henchmen, and while some training would cross over to both men and women, some was gender specific. It would be a perfect way to break the stereotypes in the field.

After the standing agenda items had been addressed in that week's HTA meeting, Matt gave Liz a quick glance to reassure himself this was the right time to introduce the possible newest addition to the HTA.

"We need to be able to wrap our heads around how to explain to the Team how they are going to be get paid moving forward. Can you explain it to them?" Matt asked.

Liz scrunched up her nose like she was a little girl trying to explain something to her parents. "I will give it my best shot. We are going to set everyone on the Team up with their own digital wallets, meaning everyone will be paid in cryptocurrency. It will be in U.S. dollars, but untraceable U.S. dollars. Everyone will be issued a credit card to use for all their bills and mortgages."

"Yes! I think you got it. We will have Jackson there too. I'm sure they will have questions. When he drops the *getting paid in cryptocurrency decentralized finance which avoids government tracking* phrase, because I can't even understand that," Matt said.

"Right! That's funny. I just know I use my card all the time, and it works just fine. Maybe that's all they need to know," Liz said.

"One last item before we adjourn for today. Liz and I have been discussing a new track to add to the HTA. One that may include Amber," Matt said.

Jimmie leaned forward and clasped his hands on the table in front of him. "This should be interesting, let's hear more."

"I think we have all agreed that having Amber come on to the HTA in some capacity is a no-brainer," Liz said. "You know I don't like her or trust her, but we do have a lot in common. But, thinking about it on a less personal level, we came up with an innovative concept. We want to create a female-specific track at the HTA. We need more of us. Between the two of us, we could turn out some phenomenal Henchwomen."

Fowler smiled. "I know you could, but who the hell do you think would be interested in it? Are there any other girls out there we can dangle this in front of?"

Liz rolled her eyes. "Nice, Dad. Of course there are others we can train! Between Amber and I, we would be able to fill those gaps. The world is changing, and there are plenty of badass businesswomen out there now. They can't always be bringing big beefy dudes with them when they don't need to be seen."

"What could be better security than to have an unsuspecting woman turn out to be a world-class trained Henchman?" Matt said.

"I would suspect that we can expect significant growth after the inaugural class graduates and gets out. How interesting indeed," Jimmie said.

"Well, you sure created a beast here. Who the fuck knew it would grow into all this?" Fowler praised.

"Before we give the go ahead," Jimmie cautioned, "let's see how she does in our mission to get the OT once and for all."

Matt received a text from Liz the next morning. "Team meeting at nine. This seems like the right time to get moving on finalizing the plan to silence the OT for good. Redhead could earn her stripes here, since she is the only one that can contact him."

Matt smiled, knowing Liz wouldn't ever call Amber by her name until her respect was earned. He responded, "That makes sense. I would like to have the OT gone for good. Will anyone else be in the meeting?"

"Franco, Jimmie, and Fowler will be present. The meeting in the conference room downstairs. See you then," Liz texted back.

Jimmie's plans to use Amber as the last piece of the puzzle in eliminating the OT, stopping his impending infringement on the DMF business model and relentless obsession with Matt, were in full swing.

The OT had been so elusive to Jimmie and the Team until now; Matt was relieved that they were finally getting some answers. On the dark web, the OT had been painted as an urban legend, with wicked fast coding skills. Jimmie wanted that rumor squashed as soon as possible.

Matt got dressed and hurried down to the meeting room.

As the Team gathered around the conference room table, Matt laid eyes on Amber. This was her first DMF Team meeting. She kept her eyes locked on her lap where her fingers were fumbling, trying to open a bottle of water. Was she hiding behind her emotions, or was the awkward shyness an act to save her own neck?

Jimmie stood to speak. "The objective for this morning's meeting is to devise a plan to take down the OT. As you are all well aware, he has proven to be cunning and elusive. With Amber's help, we feel the OT can be reached and, at long last, taken care of."

Liz, sitting in between Jimmie and Fowler, added, "The CUC had already delivered the cell phone from one of the Henchmen from the warehouse. Just to kick up the pressure on Amber, as a show of her trust to us all, she will be calling the OT right now, in the meeting on speaker phone." Liz smirked at Amber.

Amber kept a stone-face. "I'll let him know the target is my responsibility now. I'm going to inform him that I made an executive decision to let the two Henchman go due to some unprofessional behavior on the job. This guy is a total novice at the whole Henchman game, I'm sure he will believe everything I tell him."

"You're excellent at getting people to believe anything you say. I can agree with that," Matt said. Everyone at the table looked his direction when he spoke, and he noticed Amber trying to hold back a smile.

After an uncomfortable silence, Fowler turned to Amber and said, "When you call, we want you to emphasize the fact that he will get to meet Matt and tell him that you have broken Matt down. Matt is ready to tell him anything he wants to know about DMF," Fowler said.

"I understand what you need. Listen, I feel no allegiance to the OT, I'm happy to call him. He's a jerk who has it coming to him," Amber said.

Liz handed Amber the dead Henchman's phone. Amber's hand held steady as she punched in the OT's number left on the phone. The room sat silent waiting for the call to go through. Her first attempt was unsuccessful. The OT did not answer the call.

"This is typical. This guy has zero sense of professionalism. He did the same thing while we were on the job," Amber said.

The meeting continued as they briefly discussed the progress of the HTA when the sound of the Henchman's cell phone ringing quickly silenced the room. With a nod from Jimmie, Amber picked after the first ring. As instructed, she put the call on speakerphone.

Before Amber could say Hello, the OT spoke. "Who is this? I have seen your number come up more than once. Well, do you have anything to say?"

Everyone in the room appeared startled except for Amber. The looks around the room were that of confusion and disbelief. The voice Matt heard did not match the enigma of the OT. It was as if the OT was in character. The voice streaming through the phone speaker was winey, high pitched.

"Yes, I do have something to say. I'm sitting here with the Precious Prince of DMF. I thought you may want to meet him," Amber said, eyes flashing to Matt and back down to the phone.

"What? Who is this again? How did you get this number?" The OT said in an even more high-pitched tone.

"I've worked with you before. Let's just say I know why you want to speak to him. He's willing to come talk with some of his own secrets," Amber said.

Matt was impressed with how calm Amber was, despite having a room full of onlookers watching her work.

"I'm going to need a couple of days to think about it," the

OT whined. "I'm not ready to give an actual time. You can wait on me for once, Missy. Do I need to tell you to back off?"

With her best flirty, soft, calm voice, Amber insisted, "Of course you won't need to tell me to back off, I think perhaps the sooner the better would be appropriate given the situation. It has already been a couple of days, but in the end, you know what's best."

"So long as you know who's boss here. I don't need someone like you trying to tell me what to do. I'm looking forward to meeting with the Precious Prince anyway. That is the only reason I'm willing to agree to meeting tomorrow," the OT said.

"For what it's worth, I think this is a great business decision. I know that Matt has been asking about when he gets to meet you. He said he has so much to tell you about DMF," Amber said.

"I bet he does! Meet me tomorrow at the Starbucks on North Nevada Avenue, 11:00 am sharp, you know the one?" the OT said excitedly.

Amber rolled her eyes and shook her head at that comment, "Yes, I know where that is. How will I know—" Amber didn't get an answer as the OT ended the call.

"What is up with the voice? Is that for real? How fucking annoying that is?" Franco asked.

"I know, it's awful. All I can say is that every time I've spoken to him, he sounded the same and was a tool," Amber said.

"I'm ok with the timeline, but I want to know if the OT will be there alone. I wish he wouldn't have ended the call. What do you think, will he be alone or with some hired Henchman?" Fowler asked.

"That would be arrogant of him to come alone, but not unexpected," Amber said. "This guy plays by his own rules, which you have seen are anything but predictable. What you can predict is that this meeting will not be something like you had ever dealt with before. In fact, I'll place a ten-to-one odds that he will show up by himself and have an iced venti vanilla bean latte in front of him when we arrive."

There was disbelief on the faces of the guys on the Team at Amber's comment, echoed with, "I'll take that bet!" from Franco.

"So, hold on. My brain may still be a little scrambled, but did you just agree that I would do the meeting? Am I ready for something like that?" Matt asked.

"You were what I dangled in front of him to get him to meet, remember? He wants to meet you so you can spill the beans on all of DMF's secrets," Amber said.

"Sport, you will be fine. Don't you want to eyeball this little fucker, anyway?" Liz said.

"I think he will be more intimidated to meet you than the other way around," Amber said.

Matt shrugged. "Ok, I'll meet my archnemesis, but I want to figure out what the best way to handle him would be. I want to punch him in the face. I'm guessing that's not the best way to start off the meeting."

Liz smiled. "A punch in the face may be well deserved, but let's not start there. I'll help you get prepped on what to say."

"Good, thanks. I'm one hundred percent on board with getting this asshole taken care of," Matt said.

After some discussion on the logistics of the meeting, the Team also created a Plan A and a Plan B for when Matt finished the chat with the OT. Plan A would be implemented if it was determined that the OT was alone. The Henchmen would be instructed to let him get to his car, with Franco having already broken into the car and stowed in the back seat. If, on the other hand, he wasn't actually alone, then they would execute Plan B, which was to follow him, nothing more. Having a shootout in the parking lot of a Starbucks was not the way Jimmie wanted this to go down. Jimmie would make the last call to take him or not. Jimmie didn't like the attention doing business in a public place brought, especially not a place like Starbucks.

"This guy has no idea what kind of game he's playing. He's in way over his head," Amber said.

That afternoon, Liz and David H. arrived at Matt's room with pizza and beer in hand. "Are you ready to get started, Sport?"

Liz instructed Matt to engage the OT in a conversation about how deep his level of involvement in DMF was to confirm that Matt was seen as the chosen one. The strategy was to feed into the OT's eagerness to feel like he was part of the Team. If he was told confidential information by the chosen one, then hopefully that would put him at ease.

"Don't forget, it's going to be different this time. We'll be listening to your conversation the whole time. The CMs dropped off your wire for tomorrow," David H. said.

"I've never worn one, will you be able to help me get it situated in the right place?" Matt asked.

"Ha, that's right," Liz snorted, then said, "I'll be happy to show you. I think you'll be surprised how small the system is. You'll probably forget you're even wearing one."

"What if he tries to pat me down or something? I've seen that happen in movies and TV shows," Matt said.

David H. rolled his eyes. "That's right, in a TV show. This is real life College Boy."

"I don't imagine this guy is that savvy, but as a contingency plan, we'll put it in your pocket, not taped to anything. Technology has made this sort of thing a little too easy nowadays," Liz said.

"I'm not going to lie, I'm super curious to see how this plays out. There is not a chance in hell that I will stray off script. Never again, I learned my lesson," Matt said.

"Let's hope so, College Boy. I want to see who this little shit stain is, I bet it's the asshole who took a shot at Franco," David H. said.

After Liz tested the wire, Matt said, "Can you guys give me a minute? I need to gather my thoughts,"

"Go do your little-girl deep breathing stuff," David H. said.

Liz punched David H. in the arm so hard it knocked him off balance, "Fuck off," Liz said to David H. before turning back to Matt. "Gather away, we will be downstairs when you are ready. It's going to be fine, this nightmare will be over soon."

"That fucking hurt, little girl!" David H. said, turning to leaving. Liz's response to being called a little girl was yet another punch.

Deep breathing was what he knew worked best. Matt went into his bathroom and closed the door. Turning to the sink, he reached out to hold onto the side of the marble sink. Counting to himself, *one, two, three, in, hold it, one two three, let it go. You got this; this little fucker is not allowed to take any more of your time!*

CHAPTER 14
STICKING TO THE SCRIPT

AT QUARTER TO ELEVEN, the assigned Team loaded into the more inconspicuous vehicles. Matt hesitated outside the car. He wanted to spend some time alone with Amber before their meeting, but he quickly realized now was not the time to sit and have idle chat with her. Her glance back at him showed him that she was also wishing he would choose to ride with her.

"I saw that, Sport, not today. You two can hang out after this goes down, not before. You need to have a clear head. You're riding with me and David H. to lighten the tone," Liz said.

"Shit, yes, you're right, as usual. I'm wound pretty fucking tight right now. Being with you is much less pressure," Matt said.

"Is your little girlfriend going to be ok without you? Hope she doesn't steal that sweet Audi she's driving to Starbucks. You ready to go get this little shit stain? I know I am," David H. cheered.

"I'm ready. I know I can do this; I won't let you down," Matt said.

"Can you say that with a little more confidence, dude? Ouch, I'm not sure I believe you," David H. said.

"David, don't be such an asshole. He's fine, right Sport? You're going to follow the plan just like we talked about," Liz said, patting Matt's hand just as she had many months ago on their first trip to Redd's.

Matt shook his head. "I hate this guy, and I'm not intimidated by him. He's a weird little fuck. That's it, I'll be fine, trust me."

Liz sighed in relief. "This is surreal, this is the person who has shaped our world for all these months. I halfway expect this guy to have a little bravado, someone with a little flare, but after hearing his voice, I'm thinking that may not be the case."

"He's a whiney little fuck. I can't wait to eyeball his dumb ass. It will be all I can do to not beat his ass at first sight," David H. said.

The Team was on the lookout for a single male, small in stature, and perhaps showing signs of paranoia. Matt was instructed to wait in the Mercedes 450 until the OT was confirmed and the Starbucks was deemed safe.

"I think we have confirmation on the subject. He fits the description and just ordered a venti iced vanilla some shit," David H. reported to the group's text message. "He's that fucking little dude that popped Franco."

"We have eyes on him. He took a seat as far from the door as you could get, got to be him. You're right David, it's the same dude that fell on his ass when he fired the gun," Franco relayed back to the Team.

"I won the drink bet then," Amber added to the group.

"I'll settle up after this," Franco replied with a red-faced angry emoji.

Matt saw who they were talking about through the windows of the Starbucks. The OT was a little guy, young, and hardcore nerdy. He was wearing khakis and a polo that was buttoned up to the top, but the collar of the shirt was still lose around his neck. His glasses looked like they needed to be replaced years ago, with white tape keeping the arms from falling off on either side. His face was locked in a constant sneer which would lend people to believe that clearly, he had no social skills to speak of. That seemed to be his biggest downfall in this business. Just because someone was smart didn't mean they knew how the world worked.

Jimmie motioned for Amber and Matt to start walking into the Starbucks. *It's go time.*

Matt got out of the Mercedes while Amber got out of the Audi. They met at the edge of the parking lot before starting their slow walk to the door.

"We need to stop meeting like this," Amber said, breaking the awkward silence.

"What do you mean?" Matt said.

"Seems like coffee shops are our thing, you know?" Amber said.

"Oh, yeah, you're right. That, and Italian restaurants."

"Oh my, aren't you feisty today? I'll chalk that up to nerves. Are you feeling ok about all this? I think you're going to be awesome," Amber said.

"Thanks for the vote of confidence. I'm nervous, but not in the way like I don't know what to do, but nervous excited. I want this asshole to be out of my life," Matt said before holding the door to the Starbucks open for Amber.

As planned, Matt waited by the front door for Amber's cue to join the table. As Amber approached, the OT looked up with the green straw still in his mouth.

In the whiniest tone one could imagine, the OT said, "Would you please back off, ma'am? I'm expecting someone."

"I know you are. That's why I'm here, to make introductions," Amber said.

"Oh yeah, to whom? Do I know you? I don't know you,

please leave me alone. I know who I'm looking for, and it isn't you," the OT said. Amber nodded to Matt, and he made his way to the table, hands in his pockets.

The OT looked down to take a sip from his green straw, and when he looked up, Matt was standing in front of him. The OT's mouth slipped right off of the straw, causing some of the drink to spill onto the table.

"I think I'm who you're looking for," Matt said, feeling even taller than his 6'4" frame. It was all he could do to keep from jumping across the table and strangling the life out of this pathetic little man.

"Matt, yes, I'm here to meet you, finally, in person. Please have a seat," the OT motioned for him to sit at his table.

"I'll be right over here if you need *anything*," Amber said, sitting at a nearby table.

Matt knew his job in this meeting was to play the role of the bewildered victim. He was coached on how to direct the conversation. "I would say it's nice to meet you to be polite, but I'm not going there. You fucked up my life in many ways. But it was also quite helpful," Matt said.

"Helpful? How so?" the OT replied.

"Helpful in a sense that once I knew there was someone as smart as yourself following my career and involvement with DMF, I knew it was time to shift my allegiance. I know now that I'm not stuck in a dead-end company. Your interest lets me know that I have options. This was such a simple game to play with them, and thinking about working with someone like you, well, it just opened up my world," Matt responded.

Looking rather proud of himself, the OT smiled and said, "I had no idea. I wish I would've known; I wouldn't have tried to kill you."

It took Matt a split second to compose himself. His insides were burning with a desire to take the back of the OT's head into his hands and smash his face into the table several times. Instead, Matt responded, "What's in the past is in the past. We can move forward now, hopefully on the same team."

He jumped right into spilling the beans on the DMF business plan. He explained that it really was a simple plan. They created the insurance company to protect companies from their information and data being ransomed. At the same time, they were the cyber thieves that took their data and asked for ransom.

"The whole setup is basic, but very cost effective," the OT replied.

"See, I knew you were smart. I knew I wouldn't have to explain it more than once to someone like you. What a relief, some of the guys I worked with, well, let's just say, they weren't the brightest bulbs on the tree, if you know what I mean," Matt said with a wink.

As Matt finished with all the details, he could see the OT was in serious contemplation mode. The next part of the script was for Matt to tell the OT that he wanted to make a deal. Matt offered to help create the same business plan with him. It seemed to work, as the OT sat and listened to the entire plot, asking no questions. It was as if he was already setting up the system in his mind while still listening to Matt. The only movement the OT made was to suck on the green straw in his vanilla bean latte. He kept the latte right under his chin, the straw never leaving his mouth, except to sit back, stretch and process, then back to the straw.

"I'm so fucking sick of DMF. At this point, I really couldn't care less about what happens to them in the long run. I know all the ins and outs. I think I could refine the structure of their plan and make it even more profitable. I would be an asset for you," Matt said boldly.

The OT nodded appreciatively. "I know this was probably

a little difficult for you, but I want to thank you for spilling your guts to me. I always thought we would be friends and get along well. I just feel some sort of connection to you. I really look forward to working with you. Fowler and his gang should have treated both of us better."

As difficult as it was for Matt, he could agree with an affirmative nod. He wasn't sure if he could control the tone of his voice.

"So, before you go, I think it would be cool if you still pretended you were loyal to DMF. That way, as you get ready to leave and work with me, you could still collect as much information as possible," the OT demanded in his squeaky voice.

"Yeah, for sure. We will crush the competition," Matt said, trying not to grit his teeth in disgust.

Matt shot a look at Amber, as if to say, 'please get me out of here.'

The OT frowned when Amber returned to the table. "Oh, you're still here. I guess I owe you. I didn't know who you were earlier. I'll deposit the rest into your account. Whatever happened to those other two?" the OT asked.

"Didn't they tell you? They both got called to another job. They knew I would be able to handle the target, so I told them to go. You know how hard it is to find good help, right?" Amber smiled with her eyes softening and a slight tilt of her head. "Did Matty tell you I was part of the package? I mean, who doesn't need a world-class Henchman on their team? Besides, the idiots at DMF trust me now too. We will take care of things on our end. We'll be in touch. Don't look so surprised, my friend. You will be glad I'm on your side, and not the other way around," Amber said, winking at the OT.

The OT frowned, immune to Amber's charm. "No, he didn't tell me you would be joining us. I'm not sure how I feel about that. Matt, help me out here. Did she manipulate you into this?"

"Fuck no. Are you kidding me? Look, she's first class. We need someone like her, I say we keep her on," Matt advised.

Matt had been stealthily looking around the Starbucks during the meeting, and he noticed Amber doing the same. By the end of it, Matt had determined that the OT had come alone, a rookie mistake.

"I'll be in contact soon, Matt," the OT called as he waltzed past the trash can and threw his empty plastic cup at it; he missed, but he didn't stop to pick it up. Matt shook his head; he really didn't care for this guy.

"He still owes you money?" Matt asked Amber as they walked toward the door to leave.

"Yes, he does. Quite a lot of money. He was clueless when we made the arrangements. I charged him twice what the going rate was. He never tried to negotiate. He deserves what he gets," Amber said.

Matt wondered if the OT was worth saving at this point. Other than his knowledge of the cyber world, he didn't have any other redeeming qualities; would it just be easier to take him?

Matt knew the Team was watching the OT walk casually to his silver, nondescript, older model Toyota Camry. He got in without so much as a glance around the parking lot. After watching this guy in action, Matt didn't think the OT would last too long anyway in the field. Matt wondered what Jimmie's decision was going to be. Was he going to be worth the trouble in the end?

The OT backed out of his spot in the parking lot and drove down the road.

"Dude, he didn't even look around, or check the back seat before he took off," David H. texted the group. "I bet he shits himself when Franco pops up from the backseat with the barrel of a gun pressed up against the back of his head."

Matt wished he could see the OT's face when he noticed Franco in his backseat, telling him where to drive next. The OT's life was over as he knew it. Walking out of that Starbucks was the last thing he could do on his own for a very long time, karma was a bitch.

Matt and Amber quickly hopped into the SUV with David H. and Jimmie. David H. was driving and turned to Matt and said, "Way to fucking go, dude. You were awesome. To be honest, I wasn't sure what you were going to pull off in there."

"It was splendid work, I agree," Jimmie added.

"To be honest, I feel like barfing. But that's not to say I didn't feel good about it. It was so hard to not just punch him in his face," Matt said.

"I hope it didn't throw you off too terribly when I added I was part of the new team. It just seemed like the right thing to say," Amber said.

"No, that was ok. It made sense. He seemed to buy into it. He's a weird little shit," Matt said.

After a short drive, they arrived at the off-site meeting space. Liz was already there with a smile on her face.

"What's up, my friend? That was some first class bullshit you laid on him. All my work wasn't in vain," Liz exclaimed, ignoring Amber's presence.

"Thank you, and no, it wasn't. I was trained by some of the best in the business," Matt said, reaching out to give Liz a hug.

The Team turned their attention to see Franco violently pull the OT out of his car and shove his face against the back window.

"Is he fucking crying?" David H. asked.

Sure enough, the OT was whimpering with tears rolling down his cheeks. Matt had to laugh. All this time, the Team had thought the OT was a big, bad dude, and it turned out he was nothing but a sniveling little crybaby.

The OT managed to choke out through his tears, "I really meant no harm, it was all just business. Please don't kill me." He was hesitant to go first as they walked towards the empty warehouse. "I've seen movies where the guys get whacked from behind," he shouted.

Franco pushed him in the back. "Shut the fuck up, just walk. I don't want to hear another fucking word out of your mouth."

"What did I do?" blubbered the OT as he trudged into the warehouse.

No one would give him an answer. They walked silently into the warehouse. Franco shoved him in the room containing only a chair, a one-way mirror, and a lightbulb hanging from the ceiling, no windows. The others made their way to an adjacent room that had been set up to provide communication between the two rooms. The command room was equipped with a microphone, hidden cameras, and chairs. Matt assumed that this interrogation may go on for hours. Behind the glass, Matt and the others watched the OT shake with fear.

"You can't keep me here! I must get home to my fish! They need me!" shouted the OT,

"Did he just say fish? Do you really think he means that?" Matt asked. Liz shrugged her shoulders.

Through the sound system, Jimmie told the OT to have a seat in the chair and wait for further instructions. He did so, looking around the room to find any clues about his fate.

"Are you comfortable?" Jimmie asked the OT.

"Um, no, not really, am I going to die?" he trembled.

Jimmie responded, "The irony of all this is that in the end, no one gets out alive."

The OT ran his hand across his dripping nose. "I meant, me, right now, you imbecile, will I come out of the room alive?"

Jimmie waited a few seconds before saying, "It hasn't been decided yet, it depends on how you answer my questions."

"Fine," the OT whined. "What do you want?"

The first thing Jimmie, behind the one-way mirror, asked was, "Do you work alone, or do you have a partner?"

The OT spoke in a shaky voice. "I'm a one-man show. I only hire out when I need muscle or intimidation."

"How did you come to know about DMF?"

The OT replied he had been thinking of ideas on how to use the dark web to increase his business when he came across some chats about what was being done at DMF. He explored the scam from the outside in. The OT became a client. This gave him the view of the cyber security division of DMF that was invaluable. It was a test run to see if they actually did what he had heard. He embedded some code that he knew would trigger a ransom request, and with his expertise, he knew it was the same company doing both.

The one thing he wasn't sure about was how to get started. He identified some gaps and flaws in the coding. Once those were configured correctly, he figured he would just take the idea and make it his own. He had tried to get in and offer help, but the comments he made on the dark web were rebuffed, and he was laughed at. In the end, it wasn't his fault; he tried, DMF deserved to be taken over; they were disrespectful of him in a place where he had his reputation to keep.

Jimmie glanced at Matt before speaking into the microphone. "What is the obsession with Matt?"

The OT's face went bright red with anger. "It just grinds my gears that a guy like Matt, a nobody, could just become part of the DMF family for doing nothing when I tried so many times to join. He isn't smart like me. What did he have to offer?

I've seen guys like him before, good looking, athletic, semi-intelligent, life is easy for guys like him," the OT fumed, voice shaking this time in rage. Liz elbowed Matt at the 'semi-intelligent' comment. The OT continued, "Clearly, I could offer so much more to a company like DMF, even if I don't look the part of a Henchman like Matt." He practically spat every time he said Matt's name. As much as Matt could tell, the OT despised him, but Matt almost felt a little sorry for him. Though he had threatened Matt's life numerous times, he was just a confused little man desperate for a sense of community.

Jimmie looked at Amber out of the corner of his eye. "And how did you find Amber to hire?"

"Who?"

Amber smacked her palm to her forehead.

"The female Henchman you hired?" Jimmie pressed.

"Oh right, the girl." The OT rolled his eyes. "I found her on some message boards in the dark web, obviously. The places you go to when you want things done that can only be asked to do by a select few. That's where I found the Henchmen-for-hire message board, but the problem is, it never really worked out. They were mostly incompetent and untrained, probably like Matt." The OT shook his head. "I guess that's just the way it is, because really, where would you train guys like that?"

Matt thought, *the HTA, that's where.*

The OT continued, "Look, it's only a matter of time before DMF gets snagged. You have superb products in place, but if the right guy gets in and plays around, they will see what I saw. Yes, sometimes simple is better. That has worked for now, but once the others figure out the simplistic design, it will be all over." The OT had a way of rambling on. Everyone in the surveillance room was eyeing one another as the whiney voice continued talking. "I was trying to pass this important information along to you. No one listened, but I know how to fix it. You ignored me, it made me mad, I did the best I could to get your attention. I was basically jumping up and down saying, 'pick me, pick me, notice me,' and the only person you saw was Matt. Do you get it now? Can I get out of here now?" the OT whined. "I got your attention by taking the prized son of DMF, you got him back. And now you know all about me and what you are doing wrong. I think we're on equal footing, I just want to go back home and feed my baby fish!"

Fish? Why does he keep talking about fish?

Instead of completely dismissing him, Jimmie's eyes peaked with interest. Jimmie was always so unpredictable, Matt wondered what he was planning on doing with the OT. With the microphone on mute, Jimmie turned to address the room. "I think it may be a good idea to bring in a fresh set of eyes. He is no doubt annoying as fuck, but you know what they say, keep your friends close and your enemies closer. I have never thought about bringing in a rival to work with us, but this may be the right time to do that."

There were no immediate answers from the Team, just some thoughtful looks being passed around.

David H. was the first one to speak. "Is that one of those rhetorical questions?" he asked.

"No, it's not. It's a statement. We need to make this work. I want him to be part of DMF," Jimmie said firmly.

"I see where you're going with this, Jimmie. We need to include Pops on this one," Liz said.

Matt had to acknowledge that he and the OT were on the same page when it came to the modern-day Henchman needing to be trained and made more useful, but he still wasn't sure adding the OT to the Team was a good idea. "The OT wasn't loyal to anyone but himself. He has a brilliant cyber mind, one that's in tune with the current tech world, but he has no social skills, a low emotional IQ, and he's functioning at about a three-year-old's maturity level for an understanding of how people function in this world. Is he worth the risk? These are the questions we need to answer. It may open a whole new perspective for DMF," Matt added.

There certainly was a lot to think about and much for the Team to discuss. Jimmie said, "I think he's worth it. If we can get him in his comfort zone, and let him work with us, not against us, I think it would take us to new heights. I'm going to let the OT sit for a decent amount of time. There's some retribution to be paid by the guy. He's actually cost us a lot of time and money, between the security for Matt and his family and friends for these many months."

"I agree with that. Let him sit and panic for a minute. Maybe it will give him some perspective on life, although I highly doubt it," Matt said.

Jimmie added, "I've already sent an image of the OT from earlier at Starbucks to the CM Team. From that, they obtained the OT's DMV information. I also sent a couple of guys over to his apartment to see what they could find." Jimmie paused to pull his phone out and, reading the text out loud, he continued, "The report back was that the OT is a loner, has a gigantic fish tank, and massive amounts of computers and screens. Everything looked like he never left, with piles of take-out menus and clutter. No evidence contrary to who he was saying he was. The OT's name is George, George Mark Henry IV."

"Jesus, that's why he won't shut up about his little fish," David H. muttered.

Jimmie turned back to the microphone to say that the interview was over. All the 5'4," 115 pounds of George got up to leave with a sense of relief.

Jimmie continued, "I said the interview is over, I didn't say you could leave. You may as well get comfortable; you may be here a while."

"Just so you know, I'm not afraid to die! I'm angrier that you took Starbucks off my safe place to go! That was one place I could always go!" shouted George.

Jimmie, with his back to the one-way mirror, pushed the mute button. They could still see him screaming, wiping the snot off his upper lip.

"You want me to go in there and beat his ass? I would fucking love to do that," David H. offered.

"I think we should wait on that to figure out if he is going to be part of the DMF before that happens," Franco said.

"I would like to watch that, just saying," Matt added.

"The dilemma I'm struggling with is whether all of us could tolerate his personality? I believe he would be an asset but how would we be able to trust him? If he was the smartest and most knowledgeable guy, then who could keep tabs on him?" Liz questioned.

"We need to call in Max. We can let him have a go at him, let them speak the same language," Jimmie suggested.

"I'll make the call and have him brought in," Liz said, leaving the room.

CHAPTER 15
THE INTERROGATION

It would be at least an hour before Max could get to the warehouse. To be fair to George, Jimmie had the guys open the door to slide in an empty soda bottle for him to pee in, a bottle of water, and an apple Jimmie had left over.

"You know Max, correct? He traveled to Italy with you. He'll enjoy this," Jimmie said.

"Yes, I met him briefly. I've spent more time with Jackson since I shadowed him when I first started," Matt said.

"Max was a strategic hire. He's a perfect combo cyber nerd but also very personable," Liz explained. "Matt, let's go back to the House and bring him back here."

Before they left, Jimmie promised, "We won't let our guards down. I'm still not convinced that this guy is for real."

"Don't worry, dude, he isn't going anywhere," David H. said proudly.

Matt appreciated the break and was happy to get out of the small room they had been in. Matt wondered if he should ask Amber to make the trip back to the House. However, Liz gave him a look indicating that she didn't want more company for the trip. Liz and Matt arrived to find Max sitting in the kitchen, looking a bit hungover. His head was lying on his arms that were crossed on the table. When he heard them walk in, he slowly lifted his head. Though the man with graying hair had seen better days, his eyes were still kind.

"Hey Liz, great to see you. Yes, I feel as bad as I look, thanks for asking. I wasn't planning on having to work today. This better be worth my time. Jimmie seemed to think it is." Max sighed.

"You do look like shit, Max. Yes, it is important and time sensitive. We can fill you in on the way to the warehouse," Liz replied.

Max slumped in the front seat of the SUV while Liz got Max up to speed on the OT situation.

"I can see the need to get this moving sooner than later," Max noted. Exiting the Suburban, Max stumbled, quickly grabbing the hood. "Christ, I need to pull my shit together."

"Follow me, I'll point you in the right direction," Liz laughed. She held the door open for Max and Matt to walk through. They went straight to the command room.

"There he is. You look awful, my friend," Jimmie exclaimed.

"Tell me something I don't already know. Is that him? Jesus, he looks just like I pictured him. Liz, you did a good job of giving me the details. I know exactly who this type of guy is. I got this, watch me work, man!" Max smiled and pushed open the door to meet George.

"That was a quick turnaround," Matt exclaimed.

"Max is a pro, he takes business meetings very seriously," Jimmie noted.

The Team behind the glass watched as Max confidently walked into the room. George was curled up in a fetal position in the far corner of the room.

"Hey George, let's talk some shop," Max said loudly, startling little George. George uncurled from the fetal position and sat up with his back against the wall.

"Who are you? Are you here to kill me?" sniveled George.

"Think about it, George, do I look like I would kill you? I don't think I do. We have probably met before, online. My screen name is PumpkinPieLover11."

"What in the hell, that's you? I've been upset with you for a very long time! You're the gateway to DMF, and it was you who never passed my messages along. What are you doing here now?" shouted George.

"Well, George, I'm here to see how smart you really are, face to face, man to man. Honestly, they want me to confirm that you are who you say you are. Are you willing to chat with me, in our language?" Max asked.

"I guess so, but this better not be another trick like the one they played at Starbucks," George pouted.

Matt listened to the conversation as they spoke about the gaps George found. Max agreed that there needed to be greater oversight in the areas that George brought up. Matt also agreed with Jimmie's assessment that this guy's days were limited if he stayed on the same path with his far-from-charming personality. During the interrogation, Matt took mental notes of the way bullshitting was such an integral part of being a good Henchman, even the cyber guys needed to know how to layer a story with it. Adding at least one class, maybe two, at the HTA was imperative.

Max was in the room about thirty minutes before he came out to report his findings to the Team.

"Whether or not he's worth keeping long term, it's worth a shot. He's not a bad guy, just one of those entitled millennials who's too smart for his own good," Max said.

While Max had been working on George, Liz had gone out and gotten Max a large, very hot coffee.

"This is exactly what I need to keep going." Max sighed appreciatively. After taking some thoughtful sips of coffee, Max continued, "My thought is to bring him on, only on a trial basis. He knows his shit, but we need to see how he fits in. As a kind humanistic gesture, maybe we take a minute to explain things to him, about how life works and how he needs to readjust his attitude toward most things."

"Should he be given an option?" Jimmie asked.

"Sure, but let's make sure he understands that he's made a name for himself in a bad way in the 'community' as of late. But his ultimate goal is to work with us, not against us," Max replied. "Listen, I will do my best bullshitting to sell him on the notion of working with us, and not for us." He finished his coffee and returned to George's room.

"It seems you are in an interesting position here," Max said, walking behind George so he couldn't see him.

"Oh yeah, what do you mean by that? And please don't stand behind me. I know how the mob works; they kill people from behind. It is making me too nervous to speak!" shouted George.

"See, the thing is, George, I can stand wherever I want to. That's the part of being in control of a situation I enjoy. I can offer you some control if you are interested in that," Max said.

"Who wouldn't want control? You guys are still treating me like I'm dumb! I'm already sick of it, just kill me now!" shouted an impatient George.

"Hold on there, George. No one's brought up killing you, except you. Stop with that. There would only be one scenario that I can think of right now that would include you being harmed."

"Well? Spill the beans already!" George screamed.

"Does he ever just talk without shrieking? It's super annoying," Franco said to the team behind the mirror.

"Doesn't seem like it. He must have zero friends. Who could tolerate his personality?" Liz laughed.

"You sure about this, Jimmie? I could see this ending in an ass whooping from some of us," David H. said.

"He's a project in learning social norms that's for sure. How can someone be as smart as he is with computers and such an asshole to people?" Matt asked.

"Someone must have failed him along the way. I'm curious about his family. More to come on that," Jimmie said.

Max had bent down and was now eye to eye with George, so close that George shouted, "Get out of my face, old man, you reek of booze. Back off!"

"Nope, not yet. Take a big whiff of my stale air because this air is what I want you to remember each time you think of not working with us. Yes, I said working with us. I want to offer you a position with DMF," Max said, taking a step back.

George, who had been holding his breath until Max backed up said, "Ok, I get it, that smell is burned into my brain. But what? Finally, you are offering me a position. What if I say no? You don't get to use my brain anymore; offer is off the table old man!"

"You sure about your answer? I could tell you some stories about others like you who have turned down our offers, it's not pretty. Let's just say, your instincts about getting whacked from behind aren't wrong, and sleeping at night may be a little difficult for you," Max said, trying not to laugh.

The rest of the Team was laughing out loud in the control room. "There have never been any other offers, no one ever whacked in their sleep," Liz said.

"I told you I'm not afraid to die! But I will agree to come check it out. Can we end this charade now?" the OT said, finally sounding tired.

"Sure, George, think it over. We'll chat again soon," Max said.

Max came out of interrogation looking exhausted. He plopped into a chair. "I think I may be too old for this shit. Working and interrogation at this level can be challenging on a good day, but when I'm also hungover, well, that is just not cool."

"Very nice work in there, Max. If the cyber thing doesn't work out for you, let me know," laughed Liz.

"I can start with the fact that I can't call him little Georgie, I will laugh every time. How about we go with Four, short for George Mark Henry IV. He will think it very endearing that we have already given him a nickname," Max said.

"The Team will need to be debriefed on what next steps are with George, I mean Four. They need to be instructed to treat him as special, meaning, he is acting horrible because he is a scared little human," Jimmie said.

"I'm going to head back in there to deliver his fate. I'll make sure he understands it is a take it or leave it deal. Leave it meaning his dead body will be left here," Max said.

"At least no one would come looking for him. I can't imagine he has any friends!" Liz said.

Max took a couple deep swigs of coffee, grabbed his belly, and let out a long, unpleasant-smelling belch and headed back into the interrogation room.

"Here is the deal, Four. Yes, I am calling you Four from now on. The deal being offered goes like this. Upon your official arrival to DMF, you won't be given direct access to all of DMF. You will start off at the corporate offices. That way, we will be able to monitor your work. You will earn our trust. Everyone working in the DMF CM Team starts out like this. Got it?"

"So, what if I say no to you? What if I'm too good for your

stupid old DMF CM Team? I owned those guys when I was, effortlessly, by the way, hacking into your lousy firewalls. What if I say screw you?" shouted Four.

With that, Max walked over to Four, stood in front of him, and said, "Shut the fuck up. Do this, or we pour a couple gallons of bleach in your fish tanks, and we kill you right here."

"Ok, ok, I was just messing around. Playing hardball, you know, like you are supposed to do when getting a job offer? Please, don't hurt my fish!" Four shouted.

"Does anyone like you? Jesus, you are really a jerk. Anyway, I'm glad we have come to an agreement. All the guys start out with the same arrangements," Max said before leaving the interrogation room.

CHAPTER 16
LOOK UP AGAIN

THINGS HAD CALMED down where Four was concerned. After finding out he was the OT, most of the guys wanted to walk right over and break his neck and throw him out with the trash. It took a lot of convincing for them to not do that to him. Jimmie found that placating Four's infantile ego was all it took to have him be completely dedicated to the DMF cyber division.

"Heaping unhealthy doses of praise his way was all this poor little soul ever wanted." Jimmie would say. "He's undoubtedly a genius on all things cyber, and a little over-the-top ass kissing to keep him loyal to the cause was worth it in the end."

He, along with Amber, was invited to live in the DMF house after his capture and downfall. Four had been able to get attention from every person in the House in an overwhelmingly negative manner. Around the House, in the hallways, in the kitchen, everyone knew he was coming before he got there since he would have YouTube videos playing on his phone non-stop, never bothering to use headphones. He was so out of touch with any social cues, like the fact that not everyone else wanted to hear what he was listening to. The Team wondered if he had a hearing deficiency since the YouTube videos were on such a high volume. Four was always surprised when Jimmie had to ask him to turn the videos off while walking in the hallways.

Matt was surprised at how little his life seemed to change since the OT was brought in. Somehow he thought it he would feel different, less stressed maybe. What he did feel was anger. Anger that such a little social misfit was the cause of so much disarray in his personal and professional life. Punching Four in the face a few times would relieve some of his pent-up anger. That wasn't an option, or was it? If anything else, he also felt a little felt pride in himself that he did follow the plan and did a superb job in his part.

Matt received another *Look up* text and rushed to the viewing room. He hadn't received one in a while. He had just started a COD game, and he heard his team yelling at him in his headphones. "Sorry guys," he mumbled before turning his computer off. He got inside just in time to hear Amber let out a heavy sigh. She was sitting on the floor pillows beside Jimmie, absentmindedly petting Mr. Big, who was asleep in her lap.

"On top of having to navigate a new residence, workplace, and having a boss, having to deal with seeing Matt every day and pretend there are no emotions racing around us is tricky with my especially low emotional IQ," Amber said. "We have both been tentative around each other since we have been settled into the House. I'm sure that everyone can see the undeniable attraction between us. Jimmie, help me understand, why is it that I can't deal with this better? I'm usually a pro at keeping the lid on all things emotional."

"I'm not sure I'm the best to answer that for you. Like I said earlier, I am a professional emotional silencer. This may be a subject better suited for someone like Pinky to help you decipher," Jimmie replied.

Matt was confused by it all as well. He wondered how he

could be attracted to someone who was hired to kill him. He figured that it was the same way he had been able to dismiss any guilt about killing people. He had a lot more to understand about how he processed things in his life.

Amber smiled. "I'm sure Pinky would love to have some girl talk."

"Speaking of girl talk, but in a much different capacity, I think it's time that you and Liz started to work together to develop the course curriculum for HTA," said Jimmie. When Amber raised her eyebrows, he continued, "I think that you two will have more in common than not. You have had a similar sort of upbringing. I know the idea has been thrown around, but the time has come."

Amber's eyes widened and Matt noticed her body tense. "Uhm, working with Liz? Are you sure about that? I mean, I have great respect for her and the work she has done. We talked about it a while ago, but I wasn't sure if us working together would be a productive situation. When I was working on jobs, I used to hear about her, people actually compared us."

"There aren't many like you two. Liz is ready to go, and I think you should be too. I have set up a meeting for you both. I thought about being part of it as an icebreaker of sorts then decided against it. You are grown women, and I think you will be able to navigate a successful working relationship," Jimmie said.

Amber let out a dramatic eyeroll but smiled. "Ok, I'll trust you on that. I'm used to working all the time. These last few weeks have been rejuvenating and inspiring. I'm ready to get back to work. I will say that I'll miss our time together, Jimmie."

Jimmie smiled back. "Our time together is just starting, my dear. There will always be time together, just in a different shape."

Matt immediately wanted to run down to Jimmie's office,

shouting for the conversation to stop! He wasn't ready for Liz and Amber to have a one on one. He quickly texted Jimmie asking him to postpone the conversation, but it was too late.

Matt stayed in the viewing room to observe the inevitable conflict from Liz and Amber being in a room alone. Matt wondered how fast he could get down there if things escalated. Matt's stomach flopped as Liz arrived and walked into Jimmie's office.

Matt observed Amber's body language and facial expression. He saw that to a newbie like Amber, Liz was always a difficult read. Amber gave the slightest of head turn when Liz sat down on the pillows across from her. She was still going with the *proceed with caution* vibe that continued to permeate the House. Matt watched Jimmie gave Liz the *easy girl* look before he went over to his tea pot and poured two cups of green tea for the women, smiling as he offered them.

Matt watched as Jimmie excused himself so that the two women could have his office. This was strategic for the main reason that it just seemed illogical to have a negative conversation in this setting. The Zen Den oozed with peace and love vibes. Jimmie turned to look at them before shutting the door behind him and said, "I think this could end up being a really good thing."

The two women sat in silence until Jimmie had left the room.

Liz was the was the first to speak. She had mastered the *seriously, don't fuck with me* look, or as Matt had termed it, the DMF Death Stare. Those green eyes of hers made it even more intense. "I get Jimmie thinks we have so much in common. I suppose we do, on some level," Liz said, releasing some of the intensity of her glare.

Matt could see a slight pause as Amber processed how to play this forced friendship. "Yeah, well, we have both fucked some people up in a way that not many others have. I'll be honest, it's not every day I can sit in the same room and be safe enough to have a real conversation about my job, you know?" Amber had decided to pull no punches, to not be fake, and to just go for it. Matt was impressed with the bold and brave direction she took the conversation. *No bullshitting here,* he thought.

Liz simply nodded in agreement. She shifted on her floor pillow and took a sip of her tea as to say, 'go on, what else do you have to say?'

"We have a lot in common, Liz. We both know what it's like to work being the only woman in the room. There aren't many like us. We are more the same than different." Liz nodded again and Amber continued, "The biggest difference I can see so far between us is that I have done all of my work alone. I never had a team behind me. You, on the other hand, have had that, a team behind you. I don't even know what that would be like."

Liz crossed her arms and leaned back. "Hm, yeah, I would say that is true to an extent. I may have a Team, but I have also done most of my jobs alone. Being a female in a man's world can be tough. So, I agree on that point."

It was quiet for a moment until Amber said, "I mean no disrespect here, but I'm not sure how far to take the *sisterhood* conversation." Amber cocked her head to the side. "I know that you and Matt are very close."

Liz put her cup of tea down like she was ready for a fight to commence. Her face became tight with anger at the mention of Matt's name.

Matt sat forward and wasn't sure if this was the time for him to bolt out of the viewing room and forcefully take Liz out of Jimmie's office, escorting her back to his room to calm down. He wanted to hear what Amber was going to say and decided to wait, hoping Liz would allow Amber to finish her thoughts.

Amber held her hands up, palms facing Liz. "Whoa girl, I just wanted to get this conversation out of the way, it's the elephant in the room, do you agree?"

"It's the biggest fucking elephant I've ever seen," Liz said through a clenched jaw.

"I know he's your best friend, I get that, and I can see why. He certainly has a charm about him. What makes the charm so appealing is that he doesn't even know he has it," Amber said with a smile.

"Is that the same charm that kept him alive while you were actively participating in his kidnapping and possible murder?" Liz sneered back.

"Look, you and I both know how those jobs work. They work because we have been trained to not have attachments to *anything*. Am I right?" Amber asked.

Liz took a long, thoughtful sip of her tea. "And your point would be?"

"My point is that yes, it was his innocent charm that somehow was able to dismantle the iron gate that kept my emotions in check for basically my whole life. I don't even know how it happened, but it did. It freaked me the fuck out, too. I almost left the job because of it. I have never *not* finished a job. After thinking about it some, I decided the reason to stay was greater than the reason to run," Amber said.

"And what was that exactly? Your reason. I would love to hear that," Liz replied.

Amber cracked a small smile. "Well, come on, you must know. It was to keep Matt alive. I knew that if I left, his fate would be out of my hands. I knew I was more than capable of making sure he would end up alive."

"Why did you, or do you, want him alive? I've been around

this business long enough to know that motives can be self-centered, and ego driven," Liz said with her eyes narrowed.

Amber looked like she was struggling with what to say. She sighed and said, "This shit is hard for me to put into words. As much as I have seen and done, I have to admit I have a very low EQ. From what I can decipher, I do care for him. I care for him in such a way that I have tapped into a heartfelt desire to keep him safe. I want to explore more with him and spend as much time with him as possible. He brings out a part of me that's unrecognizable."

Liz sat back and leaned on the wall behind her, staring at her teacup. Matt mimicked Liz and also sat back to pause and reflect on what Amber just said. This chick was good. She either just fed them enough bullshit for them to believe and said exactly what they wanted to hear, or she had really meant it.

"I guess only time will tell whether or not Matt ends up being your prince charming," Liz replied.

Amber smiled again. "Do you really think people like us get a happily ever after?"

"I'm not sure what a happily ever after would even look like." Liz smiled back. "I think we have some work to do. The Academy is really where we are focusing our energy at this point. I'm sure that Jimmie has filled you in on what that's all about."

After hearing that, Matt's face was flushed. Maybe it wasn't an act, it was close to impossible to know for sure. Wishing it was true, a silly grin came across his face. He was glad Garrett or Franco weren't in the room to see the silly grin on his face. He wasn't ready to explain that to anyone.

Amber shook her head. "I've only been told a condensed version of the plans during one of my meetings with Jimmie. Can you get me up to speed?"

"I'm actually really excited about the progress we have made. Originally this was Matt's idea. He was, or is, a pretty terrible Henchman, but he is brilliant at seeing gaps and potential improvements."

"I can imagine from the name, the HTA, that it will involve training. I have to agree training will transform the way business is conducted. After working with some of the idiots I've worked with, I can't come up with a bad side to it," Amber said.

"We're creating a curriculum that everyone enrolled in the HTA will have to complete, then they will go into whatever track they are interested in. Once there, our vision is that they become experts in whatever sub-category of the job they chose."

"I can see you're passionate about this. What a switch for you, going from what you used to do, to this. I would love to help out. I think the concept is fantastic. I'm confident I would have a lot to offer. I'm not sure what capacity you would like to include me, but I will start wherever," Amber said.

Liz smirked. "I think pulling you in as a consultant at first would be good. Best to move slow with these guys. Besides, Matt is going to be a student there, and we don't need to have any inappropriate teacher-student relationships going on."

"He's going to be a student? That's interesting. Listen, I know I have a lot of trust building to do with the Team, but I have been thinking that I can offer some real-life shit that I've learned that would be beneficial in some of the classes," Amber said.

"At least you know that the Team still has some reservations about you being here. I'm sure as things move forward, we will be able to find a place that suits your experience and incorporate into the HTA," Liz added.

They were off to a great start from what Matt could tell. He noticed that they both looked more relaxed, and less combative.

He wasn't sure who he would place bets on in a fight. What he knew for sure was that he would most likely get his ass kicked by either of them.

"I love the idea of the HTA, but why was everything geared toward the male side of the profession? If anyone, you, Liz, should be in agreement with tailoring some of the curriculum to be gender specific. Have you ever thought about adding something for just us girls?" Amber asked Liz.

Liz frowned. "That's really fucking strange. Matt and I were just talking about that. We've already met with Fowler and Jimmie about it. If I didn't know better, I would say you were listening in to Matt and me during Taco Night."

"What would Jimmie say, there are no coincidences, right? Maybe we are on the same wavelength, or maybe I did overhear you." Amber smirked.

"I don't need games from you right now. Can we not do that?" Liz snapped.

"Oh, I'm sorry, you're right. Being cute right now isn't the best idea. Being honest, I overheard you two talking at Taco Night."

"Much better, honesty is pretty important to me right now," Liz said sternly. "So, to answer your question, yes, we are considering a Henchwoman track, but up until now, I didn't know there would be anyone to invite."

"Good point. Should we go with the *build it and they will come* motto?" Amber asked.

"I say, let's put that idea on the back burner for now. I definitely think it's worth exploring. For now, I just want to get this thing put together, get the first class graduated and see where that takes us," Liz said.

"Roger that. I would like to see this thing fly. I would like to help if you think I would be an asset," Amber said.

CHAPTER 17
ALONE TIME

THE NEXT ITEM on the to-do list was to get the key players together to go over the courses, decide who would be teaching which ones, and assign them to each instructor with the expectation that they would write up the syllabus to have ready for the next meeting. Before they could have this meeting, Matt knew there was one more in addition to the Top Five who needed an invite to the instructor's meeting.

The following day at Pinky's, Matt was at his usual spot at the front desk when Amber walked in. His stomach still did flips and flops at the sight of her. The connection they had prior to her identity reveal hadn't faded, Matt still could spend hours just staring at her. This was not the time to act like a lovesick puppy, Matt reminded himself. Instead, he needed to do himself proud, use his skills, and work on her psyche like she did to him. He was determined to find out nuggets of information that neither Liz nor Jimmie were privy to, not exactly following the advice Liz gave him. He was sensing a pattern of himself not always sticking to the plan.

It was go time as Matt approached Amber. "Hey Amber, how are you doing?"

Amber looked surprised at the greeting, but she smiled. "Hi

Matt, thanks for asking, I'm good. I have to say that this is such a different pace for me and staying in the same place this long is not something I typically do."

"I bet, big transition for you," Matt said quickly. "Listen, I was wondering if you wanted to go to our old coffee place, you know, and catch up some?"

Raising her eyebrows, Amber quickly answered, "Yeah, I would love that."

Pinky, who Matt noticed had been watching the interaction, made her way over to the desk. "Hey, you two, where are you headed, coffee? Can you grab me a nice, big, hot green tea?"

"Sure thing, Pinky," Amber said.

Pinky was already texting someone, presumably Liz, to let her know of the coffee date. "Aren't you a doll! Let me give you some money, my treat," Pinky said.

Amber reached out to pat Pinky on the shoulder. "No, we'll get it, my treat."

The two walked in silence until they arrived at the coffee shop. Matt opened the door for Amber, and as she walked past him, he smelled the familiar scent of the perfume she wore the night of his kidnapping.

"Is it strange for you to be back in here? It is for me. A lot has changed since the last time we met here," Matt began as they settled into their usual table by the front window.

"I guess it has. I'm glad it has in some ways. I ended up getting in way over my head. I know from the outside what I did looked pretty fucked up. It felt pretty fucked up. I've done so many jobs over the years, never having felt anything for the person. I look back now and wonder how I could stay so unattached," Amber said. She looked up into Matt's eyes. "I hope this doesn't make you uncomfortable, but I feel like we should clear the air about next steps with us."

"Us? You think there is still us left?" Matt asked.

Amber nodded and made a move like she wanted to grab Matt's hand, but she pulled it back into her chest. "I do. I know I have to earn your trust, but I would like to start."

Matt's original plan of gaining insights into her intentions flew out the window. First thing's first. He decided that redefining their relationship would have to happen at some point, especially if they were to work together.

"Let's start slow. Are you good with that?"

"I think that is a perfect place to start," Amber agreed, smiling.

"Perfect. Then onto the next thing I wanted to bring up with you. I know you're going to work at the HTA, but I understand that Liz spoke to you about a certain direction we wanted to take," Matt offered.

"She and I did talk about her vision of the HTA. I think Liz and I may need more time to mend fences if you know what I mean. I see so much potential in the HTA. This business needs to be upgraded into the twenty-first century. Having a female-specific portion of the HTA sound like just the right addition. That would really put us on the map. I just don't know how ready you are for that kind of attention. But long term, I think Liz and I could get things going and fill gaps," Amber beamed.

"I know you two will be able to get things going in a positive way. When you both have a common goal to work towards, I think that helps in mending fences."

"It makes good business sense. You have two of arguably the best women Henchmen in the world in one place? Come on, it would be amazing."

"If you put it that way, then yes, we would be fools to let that opportunity pass. Do you want to have another meeting with Liz, alone? How comfortable are you meeting with her now? I could be there to mediate if needed," Matt smiled.

"I'd love that. But if this is going to work, Liz and I need to figure each other's place out, just the two of us.

Matt sighed and tapped his foot nervously. "Before we head back, I have something I need to bring up with you. I don't know why I allowed myself to have any guilty feelings around you, but I do. The curse of being a nice guy, I guess. Here it goes. You know the House has a CCTV system, correct?"

"Yes, that was one of the first things I noticed when I arrived. Most places like that do. Don't forget I'm not new to this. But what about it?" Amber asked.

"To go along with that, there is a viewing room. DMF doesn't monitor it all the time, but since your arrival, it's been monitored, especially your pillow talks with Jimmie," Matt said, unable to look her in the eye.

"So what are you saying? You listened in to my talks with him?" Amber said. "Somehow that doesn't surprise me. It's fairly common to have a surveillance system in place. I knew that going into my talks with him, and I think he knew I knew. But they shared it all with you? That part I didn't know about, and now you know everything?"

"Pretty much yes, I was viewing every single one of them. I heard it all. They wanted me to feel safe, and not threatened. It was a matter of time constraints too. They wouldn't have to find time to share everything, or to decipher what I thought would be important to hear."

"Listen, my talks with Jimmie were strategic, at first. I don't think he expected anything, but as we got to know each other, they became more real, honest, and vulnerable. I was almost certain you were hearing the conversations. I hope they gave you some peace of mind," she said.

Matt's eyes were trained on the tops of his shoes, not looking at Amber is what felt safe now, "Honest and vulnerable, two words I wasn't sure would ever come out of your mouth in a conversation with me. So let me get this straight, the stuff you said about me, that was real. I need to process that. And you are right, in a twisted way it did, yes. I'm not sure why I felt the need to tell you Maybe it was to check in and see if anything you said about me, was real. Anyway, now that you know, I also wanted to invite you to the instructors' meeting. It would be good to have you there, now that you are part of the crew."

"You sure the other instructors won't mind me being there? I mean, I know I'll be a good instructor, but I'm still just the new girl here at DMF. They may not approve."

Matt shook his head, though he found himself relating to her nerves about rising through the ranks of DMF quickly. "You earned your spot there as much as the rest of them, and I'll make sure they know that."

In preparation for the instructors' meeting that was to be held in the business conference room, Matt had instructed Four to bring ten laptops to the meeting with him.

As expected, Four complained profusely at the task. "Who do you think I am, Hercules, or something? How in the world do you expect me to carry all of those? If I drop one, it isn't coming out of my paycheck!"

Matt took a deep breath before responding. "I was thinking that you may want to use one of the carts we bought just for times like this."

"Oh, well, I suppose I could use that, but still! Do you know how heavy it will be to push that? I mean really, have you looked? I am not your size!" Four squeaked.

"My bad, you're right, we can take care of the laptops,

Four," Matt said through a clenched jaw. "Liz and I will go grab them."

Four huffed off to the meeting while Matt and Liz ran to the other side of the House, through the atrium, and retrieved the laptops. Matt swore that if they were not all set up ready to use, he was going to take one and smash it across Four's face. He still hadn't completely let go of the anger he had about the damage Four had caused in Matt's life. Being the target of someone's hatred for over a year had been a bit much. He looked at Four like a yappy little dog that you were never sure wasn't going to nip at your ankles when you least expected it.

Matt and Liz rushed back to the conference room, quickly handing out the new laptops.

"Don't get up or anything, Four, we'll hand them all out," Liz said, dripping with sarcasm that Four ignored.

"Before we get started here, I want to know why she is here?" William said motioning to Amber. "I mean really. What could she possible have to do with any of this? Half the Team thinks she's full of shit," William said.

The room became quiet with everyone stopping to look at Matt. He stopped sorting the laptops to address William's question. Looking at Liz, he began to respond, "William, I don't know what we would do without your always relevant questions. Your loyalty and concern for DMF is really impressive. Why Amber is here is on the agenda, but since you asked, I will go ahead and share some exciting news," Matt said.

Amber sat back in her chair waiting for how the room would respond. Liz motioned for Matt to continue speaking.

"Golly, what could be so exciting that we get a special agenda item to cover it?" Four squeaked.

Clearing his throat, Matt said, "Amber and Liz are going to be heading up the female version of the HTA. There is a market out there for girls, shit, I mean women who want to follow in their footsteps. Not all international businesses are run by men nowadays. There are plenty of women who need Henchwomen, and we are going to provide them well trained experts."

"What the fuck. Chicks at the HTA? Dude this whole thing is so fucking weird; I guess why not. I know for a fact that both Liz and her can handle their business," Ricky said.

"William, do you have anything to say?" Liz asked.

"Nope. Maybe later I will, after I see how this all plays out. I'll call my sisters and see if they want to join," William laughed.

"Hey, it's not so bad to have your siblings working with you, right Gabe? We kinda like it," Franco said.

Since he was designated in a level above the Top Five, Franco slid into the role of their leader. He received his laptop days earlier and was being tutored by the CM Team on all the newest email and Intranet functions. With his special training, then the Top Five would be directed to come to him for questions, not the CM Team.

Amber was going to be at as many of the start-up/planning meetings as her schedule allowed. At this point, her role was to be there and observe. The rest of the Team looked at her with a mix of hostility and seduction. She could turn on her sexy Henchman aura with a blink of an eye. That had always been her go-to when she was in a tight spot. Some of the more seasoned Henchmen didn't fall for it and went with the *I don't trust her as far as I could throw her* attitude.

One by one, the Top Five—Gabe, Skippy, William, David M., and Ricky—all came to the front of the conference room table to take possession of their new company laptop. Of the five, William was the only one who looked disgusted and unenthusiastic about being handed a brand-new laptop. When William got back to his seat, he did not set the laptop down, rather he dropped it onto the glossy finished conference room table. The sound startled everyone, and all eyes turned to William.

"What the hell, man? Careful with that," Franco said.

"Oops," William grunted flatly. "What do I need this for anyway?"

Liz walked over to where William was seated and bent to meet his eyes. "I don't suppose we will have any more 'oops,' right William? That isn't how anyone should treat an expensive piece of equipment, is it?"

"No, it's really not," Four said, his nasally tone piercing the air. "Those things are sensitive, and they shouldn't be dropped like that! Jeez, have some respect."

Matt tried to hide his smile at William being chastised by Four.

William looked around and read the room. The rest of the Top Five gave him the look, the look you don't want to be on the receiving end of. The *you fucked up, don't do it again* look.

"Fuck you, Four. I didn't ask for your opinion. It won't happen again, Liz," William said. "Why is that winey little fuck here too? Since when is it common practice at DMF to let outsiders into new projects? I don't get it. Am I the only one to think this?"

"William, you are really putting me on the hot seat today. Four is here to be a representative of the CM Team. They are busy with their usual work, and Four will be working to earn his place full-time in the CM room. For now, he will be shadowing us for a bit, to get him up to speed," Matt said.

"Shadowing? That's what you call it? I'm being harassed and bothered, ALL OF THE TIME. I have no space to myself," Four cried.

"Look asshole, you brought this on yourself. If you wouldn't have been so fucking ridiculous then none of this shit would be happening with you now. Shut up and be glad you are still alive," William said.

Four knew this was the truth. Instead of trying to have a snappy comeback to William, he put his head down, pretending not to hear William's latest insult. Thankfully, all the laptops had been set up properly. Matt began going over how to use the newly created emails, the shared documents folders, all the things they needed to know to get started. None of the Team had used computers for more than gaming or an occasional email. Matt's introduction was met with a glazed over looks from the Team.

"Oh, shit. I'm sorry. We should take this a little slower. I didn't plan on spending time on this right now, but I'll schedule something soon so we can go over how to use all of the functions on laptops," Matt said.

"Thank you. I think I speak for the group when I say that none of us would be anything close to being proficient with these," Ricky said.

"I haven't ever had an email. That's how behind the times I am," William added.

Matt heard audible sighs coming from Four. "Hey, Four, did you want to say something else? Did I miss anything?"

"Oh no, you got it covered, College Boy," Four snorted like it was a funny inside joke, pushing up his glasses with his middle finger. No one had called Matt College Boy for months, and no one at the table laughed except for Four.

Even the death stare from Franco didn't get Four to notice that what he said wasn't funny or appropriate. The rest of the Team just rolled their eyes and proceeded to the next section of the meeting. The next section was designed to let everyone know who would be leading each of the subjects. It had been predetermined that before the Top Five could teach, they would have to complete their leadership training.

The training was a little something Matt put together from research he had done. He wanted to make sure that the information wasn't too difficult to comprehend. He wanted the Top Five to feel successful and to be able to participate in the discussion. The concept of leadership had never been properly addressed as Henchmen. Matt wanted it to be an organic selection process, where the smarter or more outgoing guy on the Team eventually became the lead. This training would help them the rest of the Team have tools to use when in tense situations, where dialogue would be chosen over death or injury to the parties involved.

From this initial instructor meeting, the classes were assigned to each leader. Ricky would instruct classes from both the HTA and the shooting range that was just outside of town. The main focus would be to teach students how to properly hold a firearm.

William's class focus was on wire explosives and the science behind the behavior of fires. Though most of the classes would be outdoors, William would also have some classroom instruction. William was the most quiet and unassuming of the Top Five, which led Matt to want to keep a closer eye on how he fared through the leadership training.

Gabe, the fighting expert, would have his own classroom at the HTA. Strategically, there were no hallway windows in the combatives room. This was for a couple of reasons, one being they didn't want anyone thrown through a pane of glass, the other being that Gabe assured everyone that most classes would involve blood, which may cause anxiety to people looking in from the outside.

Skippy, the getaway driving instructor, thought it best to conduct most of his classes in the vehicles that the Henchmen would drive to the HTA and park in the back.

David M. admittedly struggled with how to teach a class on

bullshitting. He had trouble articulating how it was done. "I just do it, and don't think about *how* I do it."

After some discussion, the team came up with watching David M. work people out in public and to have him to role play with them. "I'll serve up a big plate of smug bullshit and see if they would be able to work their way out of it. Once they could successfully navigate that, then they would in turn be the bullshitter in the subsequent role plays."

Matt was particularly fond of the way he learned about being a Henchman. When he first started, Jimmie required him to watch training videos. Matt found this exercise to be very helpful. Liz had created a list of over thirty movies that included all types of Henchmen. It gave Matt insight as to "good" Henchman, and what made them "good." In Matt's opinion, the best of the best were Henchmen who never spoke, knew exactly what their roles were, and never went off script. All the lessons that Matt had to learn the hard way when starting out. Watching the movies, and then having a class discussion would be a great way to introduce them to the HTA. It was agreed upon by the Team that this was the class where the five rules of being a Henchman would be introduced, having them commit to memory before they would be considered to have passed the class. As a joke, Liz asked Matt to recite the five rules since he had such trouble with them as a newbie Henchman.

"Ha-ha, very funny, Liz. Four, you better take notes on this. These are the five rules we live by. One, never speak on the job. Two, never run an errand on your own. Three, never argue with an order. Four, never hesitate. Five, know your role, stay in your lane. How's that?"

"Ok, ok, you got it going on, good for you," Liz said with the room chuckling.

"What is that supposed to mean? Run an errand, I don't get it," Four whined.

"You will figure it out in time, but for now, just remember rules one and three for now," Liz said with more chuckles from the rest of the room.

Franco would be assigned as a mentor to each of the Henchmen entering the HTA and tasked with developing an interpersonal relationship with the newbies. He was to get to know them better, learn about their likes, dislikes, home life, their past, what their goals were, how they got to HTA, make it personable. He would also share with them parts of his life and how he was able to achieve the status he had with DMF. It was Matt's idea that if there was a more friendly atmosphere, and the Team knew each other on a personal level, they would strive to perform on a higher level. With the ranking system in place, he would be the first to give them an official lapel pin to designate their status level.

Amber was not slated to teach a class in the first round of classes. She would observe and take notes discreetly about the progress of each new Henchmen. She would be there as a sort of distraction to them, her presence never being explained to them, but looking innocent and coy while roaming the halls of the HTA. Amber had shown a mastery of the art of stealthily compiling loads of information.

Liz and Jimmie were working together to create the "holistic" section of learning at the HTA. Liz had wanted to create a support group from the inception of the HTA. The most challenging thing about being a Henchman was the lack of the ability to process what went on in her life and her career. Jimmie had taught them well how to stuff emotions, feelings, of any sort deep down. He had given them all the ability to consciously justify ending people's lives. Those skills helped them all to survive on a surface level. Liz wanted to have a forum for them to all talk about their shared experiences of being a Henchman. Liz knew that there would be all levels of disclosure and processing, some wanting to, some not even comprehending that what they did was seen as not ok. Liz had been seeing a therapist for years, which was the only way she had been able to live through the continual stuffing of her feelings. She was bound and determined to create a safe open place for discussion.

"Why would you want to sit around and talk about your *feelings?* What a bunch of babies," snorted Four.

Liz stood up and made her way over to where Four was sitting. The room watched her as she arrived at his seat. Four pretended that he hadn't noticed her getting up and walking towards him by keeping his eyes trained on his phone.

"What do you want? Why are you standing over me like that? Back off, *Liz,*" Four sneered.

"Stand up you little fuck, right now," Liz demanded. The room was anxiously waiting to see her tear him apart.

"Why would I do that? Are you going to try and kick my ass or something? I wouldn't suggest doing that, your daddy may get upset with you," Four said through squinty eyes.

"Stand up right fucking now you little piece of shit," Liz again demanded.

Four would not move. He turned away from her, spinning his chair in the opposite direction.

"Hey asshole, I would just stand up if I were you. She's not one to take a joke like this," Franco said.

With that, Liz grabbed the back of Four's chair and spun it around so quickly that he flew onto the floor. Four landed on his chest so hard that his glasses had fallen on the floor just in front of his face. Liz walked over to the glasses and placed her foot on the top of them, not yet stepping all the way down on them. Four looked up with fear and anger in his eyes.

"Hey! Watch it, don't step on those! I need those!" yelled Four.

"Fuck off. I have about as much respect for you as I do these stupid, ugly glasses. You are nothing to me, I can squash you just like these glasses. Do you understand? Don't talk to me or make any sort of comment to me or about me. I will crush you, and I don't give two fucks what my daddy has to say about it," Liz said, bringing her foot down on the glasses, crushing them into pieces.

"No! My glasses!" Four shrieked. He began to form the words bitch when he looked around the room and saw that no one was laughing. For once, he learned when to shut his mouth. Four gathered what was left of the pair of glasses, stood up to grab his laptop and notes, and left the meeting without another word. As the door shut behind him the rest of the room quietly laughed their asses off.

With the slam of the door, Jimmie magically appeared in the room. He took a quick glance around, noticing that there was an empty seat. Raising his eyebrows, Jimmie addressed the meeting, "Four? What did he do this time?"

"Liz was just about to whip his ass," Matt said with a half-smile.

"I didn't, but I sure wanted to fuck him up, Jimmie. I just stepped on his glasses. He's a blind little fucker right now," Liz said with a huff.

"Christ, I better get up there and see what he needs to do to get new glasses," Jimmie said. "Matt, does Four have his insurance active? Can he use that to get a new pair of glasses?"

Matt nodded. "He was set up with the whole package, which includes vision coverage. Let him know that he can log onto the policy to see what optician will take our insurance."

"Well, good for you for not breaking his neck, Liz." Jimmie winked and left the room to go find Four.

CHAPTER 18
THEN THERE WERE THREE

Because Four had left the meeting, Liz texted Jackson to attend in his place. No one really thought Four would make it, socially, in the instructors' meeting. Jimmie wanted to give him an opportunity to be one of the guys. Jackson was on standby, knowing that was highly likely that he would be called in to replace Four.

"That didn't take long, what did he do, or should I say who did he piss off?" Jackson said upon his arrival to the conference room.

"He was an asshole to Liz," Matt explained.

"Oh, not good. Where are we at then?" Jackson asked.

"We wanted to let the instructors know where the CM Team was on getting the HTA online, and if you had been able to find anyone that is here already to start with the cyber intel portion," Liz said.

"There's no one currently on the team that would be anywhere near ready to start learning the level of cyber intel needed to be effective. Whoever is selected for the cyber track of the HTA needs to not only be well versed in the navigation of the dark web, but they also need to have the patience of a saint to work with Four on a daily basis," Jackson said.

There was a discussion about how critical it was for DMF to have a robust cyber division, as cyber-crimes were the way of the future. It made all the Henchmen in the room roll their eyes when they realized that Four would be classified as a Henchman.

"He just doesn't deserve the title of Henchman," Franco said, shaking his head. "He gives us all a bad name. It amazes me that he hasn't pissed someone off enough that they haven't wiped him off the face of the earth."

"For what it's worth, from the little I know of him, he pretty much never left his house. He ordered everything online, food delivered, worked remotely. I think that is the only reason he has made it this far," Amber said.

As she spoke, the whole room turned to look at her. She had been silent through the meeting, only offering slights nods of agreement or understanding. Matt looked at her and could not stop those feelings from bubbling back up to the surface. *Get a grip man, she is still on your shit list, remember!*

The way the other Henchman in the room looked at her, he could see why she was so good at her job. She had a way about her that when she spoke people wanted to hear what she had to say, almost as if they became entranced with her. She knew it too; she knew the outright power she could have over people in a matter of seconds. Someday Matt wanted to ask her if she had used her magical charms to seduce him into a blubbering idiot, those charms that no one on the DMF Team was able to see through.

Liz cleared her throat loudly to turn eyes away from the mesmerizing Amber. "Sport, I wanted to ask you if you knew anyone from your past gamer life who could be a good fit for the CM Team? I know there must have been some hard-core nerds that came into The Basement. Maybe some of them would be willing to give up their regular gig and hop onboard with DMF?"

Matt sat back in his chair, "Shit, I didn't think about that, but yeah, I suppose I think about touching base with someone from there. I haven't been there since, well, you know, that night. Let me think about that and get back to everyone about that."

"Well, if not them specifically, maybe they would know someone that would work," Liz said.

"If someone from The Basement doesn't work out, maybe we can ask Four if he has any friends, or knows someone," Matt said with a wink.

"Oh, I'm sure he has a lot of friends!" Liz snorted.

The Team stood and gathered their new laptops and papers as the meeting adjourned. They had agreed to work on their assignments and to meet the same time the following week. It made Matt feel like a bit of a success when he heard Skippy say to William that that was the first time he had ever been in a 'real' meeting. He had always wondered what it would be like to be important enough to be included in a meeting. That was exactly how he wanted this to be, a first for them, and to show them their value as part of the inner workings of DMF.

Matt had made plans with Amber and Liz to meet first thing in the morning in the kitchen after the instructor meeting. They had table number one reserved.

Liz sat down at the table with coffees and Matt's favorite donuts.

Matt wasn't sure if he was going to have to be a mediator. He was anxious wondering if he would have to break up a fight.

"Hey Billy Badass, way to crush Four's glasses. Nice work, that was classy," Matt said.

Liz smiled. "It was pretty fucking funny. He just makes you want to punch him in his face every time he opens his mouth."

"It's amazing he's stayed alive as long as he has. I'm surprised no one has wasted him," came Amber's voice from behind them. She stood awkwardly near the table until Matt offered her a spot beside him.

"He's been one lucky SOB," Liz agreed, eyeing Amber as she sat down.

Once the three were sitting in the same room, intense energy could be felt as the two women visually sized each other up. Matt knew he would more than likely have to be the director of the meeting to ensure it was productive.

"Thanks for meeting with us, Amber," Matt began, "I don't think we need to rehash anything do we? Are you both ready to put the past behind us and reset?"

Liz shrugged. "Works for me. I find holding grudges is a waste of time. I think she knows I have some respect for her work, but that I'll have my eye on her a bit longer."

"I would like a start fresh, as fresh as possible given the current situation," Amber chimed in, turning to Liz. "Liz, you know how jobs go. I did mine, but I'm also ready to let go of my past. I don't want to sound whiny or cheesy, but I don't have anywhere else to be right now. I would like to be part of something bigger."

Matt smiled at their civility. "That's a good place to start. Let's jump right into it. Like we discussed, I wanted to let you know we have a green light from leadership at DMF to develop a new Henchwoman track. This won't happen right away, but it's something we want to eventually incorporate into the structure of the HTA."

"The HTA is a huge endeavor for us to prepare and plan

for. It's hard to wrap our heads around possible expansion before we even open the doors. I hate to admit it, but you and I could really develop something amazing for those up and coming," Liz said.

Amber nodded. "I agree. If you hadn't already mentioned this, I was going to. It seems like a natural way to expand."

"To begin, we would like you to help with the course development and to possibly help teach some of the classes. Once we have things going, we would like to investigate opening up a section for the addition of a girls-only track," Matt said.

Liz frowned at Matt. "Girls? Are you serious, did you just refer to us as *girls*?" she scoffed. "Either one of us could take you in hand-to-hand combat. We would whip your ass before you even saw it coming."

Matt felt his cheeks burning as Amber hide her smile behind her hands. "Sorry, that's not what I meant, and I know you could inflict some serious damage, I know first-hand both of you can hit like a boy. We can come up with the name of the *female* track of the HTA closer to the start of it, how does that sound to you both?"

"We'll have to, or none of the badass women we want to come will show up," Amber laughed. "And can I just say, I'm humbled and excited to be part of this. I don't know if you can comprehend the impact this will have, globally."

Matt was glad conversation was going well. It seemed like Liz was happy to have another female on the Team and thought it was great to balance it out. Amber and Liz bonded over similar experiences they had, nothing that either of them had ever done before. It made him cringe when the two Henchwomen would talk about what idiots men could be.

"I swear, a low-cut shirt, push up bra, tight pants, and batting your eyelashes are the only weapons you need on a job," Amber laughed.

"Yes! And playing really dumb and complementing them. Combine all of those, and they are toast!" Liz chuckled.

"My go to is asking them for help. They love that shit. 'Can you help me open this jar? Can you help me fix this broken picture frame?' Blah blah blah. Stupid men are no match for pretty girls," Amber said.

"Amen to that. It's kind of sad sometimes, how they are so easy to maneuver. But not really! It's fun now. How are we going to teach this at the HTA? Flirting Skills 101," Liz suggested.

"You two are brutal. Are men really that ridiculous when it comes to beautiful women?" Matt asked.

"One hundred percent," both Amber and Liz said in unison.

"Ouch. I never thought I would say this, but I'm starting to feel like the third wheel," Matt said.

"Let me back up here a minute though. From the first night I met you, you showed me respect and did not look at me like I was a piece of meat. It took me a minute to figure out what was different about you, why I felt at ease with you. I never felt uncomfortable with you," Liz said.

"He does have that charm going for him, I will say that. You can be our third wheel anytime you want, right Liz?" Amber said.

Liz nodded in agreement.

"Well, thank you, ladies. I'm relieved to know that I'm not classified with the rest of my gender as some misogynistic pig," Matt said, rising to his feet. "It seems like I don't really need to be here anymore. I'm going to Pinky's to work out, I need to burn off some anxious energy. Anyone want to come with me?"

Liz and Amber shared a shy smile.

"No, I think I'll stay here for now. Enjoy being able to drive yourself now. It's what you've been waiting for all this time," Liz said, smiling.

"I'll stay here too, if Liz is cool with that?" Amber said, looking to Liz, who nodded. "See you later, Matt. Have a good workout."

Matt quickly ran up to his room to change and grab his bag. He could hardly believe his eyes. His best friend and his sort-of-ex-girlfriend were actually getting along.

On the drive to Pinky's, he reminisced about the first time he went to Pinky's and how different things were back then, just a few months ago. Since he wasn't working on the HTA, he parked out front of Pinky's. *Just like old times*, he thought.

He was in such a good mood, he felt so relaxed as he climbed out of the black Audi, whistling the song he had just been playing in the car.

Matt turned to walk into Pinky's when two men in suits approached him. They took Matt by surprise, taking him a second to realize they were not any Henchmen he knew. They grabbed him before he could even drop his bag to fight them off.

"*Per favore, Signore*, come with us," said the navy suit.

"No fucking way! Are you kidding me? I'm not going anywhere with you!" shouted Matt, struggling to get free.

"*Per favore*, don't make things *difficile*. Someone would like to have a word with you," the navy suit said.

Their grips were so strong, and quick, he didn't have a chance to argue. Within seconds, he was forcefully thrown into the backseat of a black Range Rover.

"What the fuck? Who are you? What do you want?" screamed Matt, fumbling while trying to open the door, only to find out the door handles had been removed.

With a thick Italian accent, the mysterious man said, "You don't recognize me? I am surprised, I thought you had better observation skills than that."

Matt's eyes had now adjusted from the bright sun outside to the darkness inside the Range Rover's tinted windows. He could now see clearly that the man who had kidnapped him, this time, was Vinicio Rossi, the Italian connection from his first overseas trip with Fowler.

"It's you. What is this shit?" Matt demanded.

"There you go, I would have been insulted if you hadn't been able to place me. You can calm down now. I am just here to ask you a few questions," Rossi said in too calm of a voice.

"I doubt calming down is an option for me right now. I've been through this shit before. I'm not sure if you know Jimmie, but he will come for me. You're not playing with a rookie team, dude," Matt hissed.

Matt tried to discreetly look around for ways to get out of this mess, cursing himself for not having a gun on him. He was trying to move away from being that guy, the one who was always carrying. He didn't want to make that his permanent identity. He thought he was safe now that the OT was no more. *Why is this Rossi character to interested in me?*

It was hard to be a total asshole, since Rossi exuded class and appeared to be the ultimate gentleman. If anyone were to see him on the street, he would present as a very rich, confident man. Matt thought *his* suits were nice, the suits these Henchman had on were on a different level of fine fabric and tailoring. Matt noticed Rossi even smelled good, a scent he had never smelled, but in a strange way made him want to know more about him.

Rossi had a smug grin on his face that said he was going to ignore the Jimmy threat. "I have some questions for you about this HTA business. This is your idea, your work, correct?"

Matt shrugged. "The HTA? Yeah, why do you care? It has nothing to do with you."

"That is where you are wrong. I want to know why you

think it is necessary to change an ancient system that keeps men like myself safe. What is it they say here? 'If it ain't broke, why fix it?'" Rossi said, leaning forward.

"Are you serious? It *is* broke. Have you seen how these guys work? I'm just making things better, less financial drain, less collateral damage, shit like that. Guys like you will still be safe," Matt said.

"Can you honestly say that if you and your Team were, as you say, given the job to go pick someone up, that it would have been done with as much grace, and non-violence as these two gentlemen showed you?"

"Well, maybe not. I was worried about my nose being broken again. It has just healed from being broken the last time I was kidnapped."

"Perfect example. You will be able to see more examples once we reach my villa. I heard you like to fly in private jets," Rossi said, smiling.

Matt hadn't noticed that the Range Rover had stopped when suddenly the doors opened, and he was ushered out to the steps of Rossi's jet.

"Welcome to *my* world, Matt."

ALSO BY L.K. URBAN

The Henchman Training Academy 1: Evolution

If you haven't already, find out how Matt got involved with the Henchmen in book 1 and began the Evolution!

Coming soon, ***The Henchman Training Academy 3: Extraction***.

The HTA goes global . . . only time will tell if that is a good thing or if it will be the last thing the HTA does. Book 3 coming soon.

Keep reading for an exclusive sneak preview of Book 3!

NOTE TO THE READER

Dear reader,

Thank you for taking the time to read book 2 of The Henchman Training Academy.

If you are wondering about how Fowler and Jimmie met, or wanting to know more about Matt, Liz, Amber, Franco, or anyone else, sign up for my monthly newsletter to receive more character backstories, and other adventures of the DMF Henchman Team. Visit LKUrbanAuthor.com to join the HTA.

It would mean a great deal if you could leave me a review on Amazon and Goodreads, and of course, spread the word.

Remember, listen to that quiet voice that is whispering to you. Follow it, see where it takes you, this is your truth, speaking to you. It is always there; we just don't hear it after a while.

Follow me @LKUrbanAuthor on Facebook, @LKUrban-Author on Instagram, and @LKUrban on TikTok for more content.

With love,

L.K.

ABOUT THE AUTHOR

L.K. Urban is a dreamer, writer, and adventurer.

When she is not on the road traveling around the United States in her burgundy Mini Cooper (affectionately named Ron), L.K. lives in beautiful Colorado Springs, Colorado, close to her four wonderful children.

Upon becoming an empty nester and entering into the pandemic of 2020, L.K. became one of many quarantine writers. Thanks to COVID, her first series, *The Henchman Training Academy*, was born and fulfilled her lifelong dream of becoming a published author.

In addition to being a creative, L.K. also holds a license as a Marriage and Family Therapist and is a working practitioner.

You can find her at:

LKUrbanAuthor.com

Or find her on social media.

facebook.com/LKUrbanAuthor
instagram.com/LKUrbanAuthor
tiktok.com/@LKUrban

EXCLUSIVE PREVIEW: THE HENCHMAN TRAINING ACADEMY 3: EXTRACTION

CHAPTER 1

Rossi's private jet was a reflection of himself, first class in every detail. Rows of black leather oversized chairs filled the cabin, highly polished chrome sparkled in the bright sunlight. The flight crew looked as though they stepped out of Italian Vogue, all with matching well tailored navy suits, ruby red neck scarfs, black stilettos and impeccable hair and make-up. This aircraft was larger than Fowler's, which Matt was blown away by. *This is fucking incredible.* Matt shook his head in disbelief because one, he had been kidnapped, yet again, and two, because if anyone was going to be kidnapped, this was one hundred percent the way to go—in this magnificent private jet, on his way to an incredible Italian villa.

At least he assumed that was where they were headed. Rossi and his team of Henchmen had only spoken Italian since they'd taken off. Matt's phone had been taken from him as quickly and gracefully as he had been thrown into the Range Rover outside of Pinky's. *Shit, it had all gone down so quick, what could I have done differently*? Would a class at the HTA on how *not to be kidnapped* have helped? Maybe just being more aware of his surroundings was more like it.

Months ago, when the OT's Henchman for hire tried to

kidnap or kill him in almost the same spot, all three of them, Matt, Franco and David H. hadn't been paying attention to their surroundings. This time, Matt's guard was down, the OT was not a threat anymore, he just wasn't expecting this, at all.

To continue reading the exclusive sneak preview of first chapter, sign up for the newsletter at LKUrbanAuthor.com.

www.ingramcontent.com/pod-product-compliance
Lightning Source LLC
Chambersburg PA
CBHW021137190726
48288CB00008B/2694

* 9 7 8 1 7 3 6 4 5 8 2 7 3 *